Teacher's Pet

To Julie, with thanks for everything

Acknowledgments
Thanks to Judith Tamas, D.V.M., Kim Michels, D.V.M., and Melissa Campbell
and the staff of The Seeing Eye in Morristown, New Jersey. Thanks also to James
Hughes and Ronnie, of Long Island, and the terrific people at Overbrook School
for the Blind in Philadelphia.

Please visit our web site at: www.garethstevens.com
For a free color catalog describing Gareth Stevens Publishing's list of high-quality
books and multimedia programs, call 1-800-542-2595 (USA) or 1-800-387-3178
(Canada). Gareth Stevens Publishing's fax: (414) 332-3567.

Library of Congress Cataloging-in-Publication Data

Anderson, Laurie Halse.
    Teacher's pet / by Laurie Halse Anderson.
      p. cm. — (Wild at Heart)
    Summary: Adjusting to middle school becomes easier for twelve-year-old Maggie when
she finds that her biology teacher, who is blind, can learn a few things from her about working
with his guide dog.
    ISBN 0-8368-3261-2 (lib. bdg.)
    [1. Guide dogs—Fiction. 2. Dogs—Fiction. 3. Blind—Fiction. 4. People with
disabilities—Fiction. 5. Teacher-student relationships—Fiction. 6. Schools—Fiction.
7. Veterinarians—Fiction.] I. Title.
PZ7.A54385Te   2003
[Fic]—dc21   2002036518

This edition first published in 2003 by
Gareth Stevens Publishing
A World Almanac Education Group Company
330 West Olive Street, Suite 100
Milwaukee, WI 53212 USA

First published by Pleasant Company Publications, Middleton, Wisconsin.
Original © 2001 by Laurie Halse Anderson. Illustration and design © 2001
by Pleasant Company.

American Girl® and Wild at Heart™ are trademarks of Pleasant Company.

Cover Photography: Brian Malloy
Newspaper Clipping Photography: Jamie Young

Photo Credits: cover—German shepherd courtesy of Wisconsin Academy for Graduate
Service Dogs; pages 133, 134, 136—Guide Dogs for the Blind, Inc. www.guidedogs.com;
pages 135, 137—© J.T. Miller, 2000

Although Ambler, Pennsylvania, is a real town (a wonderful town!), the setting, characters,
and events that take place in this book are all fictional. Any similarity to real persons,
living or dead, is coincidental and not intended by the author. This book is not intended as
a substitute for your veterinarian. Your vet is the best source of health advice for your pet.

Printed in the United States of America

1 2 3 4 5 6 7 8 9 07 06 05 04 03

American Girl®

Teacher's Pet

Laurie Halse Anderson

Gareth Stevens Publishing
A WORLD ALMANAC EDUCATION GROUP COMPANY

ONE

"Anybody want a water ice?" I call through the screen door of the Wild at Heart Animal Clinic.

"Water ice!" several voices shout from inside. Chairs scrape the floor, file drawers slam shut, and a stampede heads my way. Water ice—shaved ice drenched with flavored syrup and pieces of fruit— is a summer favorite around Philadelphia. Totally yummy.

David Hutchinson bolts out the door first, fol- lowed closely by Brenna Lake, Sunita Patel, and . . .

"Where's Zoe?" I ask. My cousin loves water ice. I bought the mango just for her.

"She's shopping with your grandmother," Sunita says as I hand her the cup of watermelon ice and a plastic spoon. "Thanks, Maggie!"

David grabs the chocolate water ice out of my bike basket. Brenna takes the grape, and I take the strawberry-kiwi. I lean my bike carefully against a tree, then join the others sitting on the steps of the clinic.

"I can't believe she's shopping *again*," I say. Zoe's goal is to have a different outfit for every day of the year. Me, I'm happy in shorts and a T-shirt. And basketball sneaks, of course.

Brenna puts an enormous spoonful of ice in her mouth. "Cool pies," she mumbles.

"Huh?"

She swallows. "School supplies," she repeats. "Dr. Mac took Zoe shopping for paper, pens, and notebooks. They were going to take you, but you got back too late."

"I wasn't gone that long, was I?"

Sunita checks her watch. "Almost two hours. Where did you go?"

"All over the place," I say as I unbuckle my bike helmet and toss it on the grass. "I rode around the park, I shot some hoops, then I wandered down Main Street. I wanted to look at everything one last time. Because of . . ."

I can't say it. The words stick in my mouth.

"School," David finishes for me. "Because of school starting tomorrow."

"Middle school," I correct him.

"You aren't psyched to go back?" Brenna asks with a puzzled look on her face.

"You're kidding, right?" I reply. "I just got used to sixth grade! Now we have to start all over again. I wish it could be summer forever."

Something scratches at the clinic door. David opens it, and my chubby basset hound, Sherlock Holmes, ambles out. He walks over to me, puts his heavy head in my lap, and sighs.

I laugh and pet his sleek fur. "You know how I feel, don't you, buddy? Too bad I can't take you to school with me."

"Cheer up, Maggie. It'll be great," Brenna says confidently. "We'll meet lots of new friends."

"Friends aren't a problem," I explain. "Teachers are. Last year I just had to deal with Ms. Griffith. Now I'll have a different teacher for every subject. What if they all give me homework on the same night? I don't want to go."

To be honest, it's more than just teachers. I know I can't read as fast as other kids. Math is hard, too. What if I'm not good enough, not smart enough? What if I fail? It's only going to get harder from here on out.

Sherlock Holmes yawns loudly and stretches across my lap, his belly up. What a dog! He can always tell when I'm bummed.

"Thanks, buddy," I tell him as I scratch his tummy.

"He's telling you to chill," Brenna says. "Middle school is just like elementary school, only bigger."

Sunita twirls her spoon in her cup. "Maggie's not the only one who is nervous."

"You, too?" David exclaims as he turns to her. "Why? You're smarter than most of the teachers!"

"Well," Sunita says slowly, "I'm worried about my locker."

"Your locker?" Brenna asks.

Sunita nods. "What if I can't open it? What if I can't remember the combination to the lock? If you're late for class, you get a detention. And the halls are really crowded."

Brenna licks her spoon with a purple tongue. "Don't worry. Your locker will work perfectly. And the halls are never crowded. My brother promised me."

"And you believed him?" I ask. Brenna's older brother likes to play practical jokes on her.

She pauses. "Good point. He *was* acting a little weird when he told me that—all friendly and nice. But I'm not going to worry about it. Today is the last day of summer—of the best summer ever. I'm going to enjoy it."

She's right. This summer rocked. We worked at Wild at Heart, taking care of animals big and small, rescuing pets from a hurricane, and walking all kinds of dogs. But best of all, we really got to know each other.

Brenna is the most like me in the group—sort of bossy and very opinionated. She's crazy about wild animals. When we were in Florida, she jumped into a canal to save a baby manatee. I hope she's in some of my classes this semester. She would be a great project partner.

Sunita gets the vote for "most likely to be reading a book." She's my main girl for homework help. Along with books, she loves cats. It's like she can understand what they're thinking. (I once saw her calm down a Siamese cat freaked out by a hurricane!) I love having her around the clinic.

I've known David forever. He lives across the street. I used to think he was a real goofball, but underneath that ridiculous haircut is a good guy. David proves that boys love animals just as much as girls do. He is especially nuts about horses. Thanks to him, we all had riding lessons this summer. We also shoveled a lot of manure.

Even Zoe had a good time this summer. That's good, because she's going to be here for a while.

Her mom, my aunt Rose, is trying to get a part in a television show in Hollywood. She's too busy to take care of Zoe right now. Zoe talks a lot about being the daughter of a famous actress, but I think she likes being a normal kid better. She's finally trained her mutt, Sneakers, and she's the best phone answerer we've ever had at the clinic.

David wanders over to my bike and takes the mango water ice out of the basket. "It's starting to get slushy," he says.

"You can eat it if you want," I say. "Knowing Gran, they probably stopped to get some of their own. Gran loves the cappuccino cream flavor."

David doesn't need any more encouragement. He tilts his head back and gulps down half of the ice at once. Then he staggers a step and clutches his head.

"Brain freeze!" he groans.

We bust out laughing. "Press your tongue against the roof of your mouth," I say. "It sounds weird, but it works."

"Won't help," Brenna teases.

"His brain has been frozen for years," Sunita adds.

David scowls at them, but he can't say anything. He's too busy thawing his brain.

Sherlock raises his head off my lap and lets out a deep "Woof!"

Gran is home.

As she's parking the van, Zoe sticks her head out the window. "We got the coolest stuff!" she shouts. "Purple notebooks, gel pens, book covers, index cards, calculators, staplers, and tape. We bought out the whole store!"

Yippee.

There's only a little ice left in my cup. I tilt my head back and tap the bottom of the cup.

"I can't *wait* for tomorrow!" Zoe says dramatically as she runs over to join us.

Splat! The strawberry-kiwi water-ice clump slides down the side of the cup and smacks me in the face.

I can.

TWO

As Zoe heads to the kitchen to unpack her goody bag, a sputtering red Jeep parks next to Gran's van. The doors open, and the Donovan family pours out: Shelby and Inky, twin black Labrador retrievers, along with Christopher and Nicholas, energetic three-year-old human twins. Poor Mrs. Donovan, who always looks tired, closes the doors and grabs the dogs' leashes.

Shelby and Inky helped bring our group of volunteers together. The puppies were rushed to Wild at Heart last spring. They had been bred in a horrible puppy mill and were close to death. They're completely healthy now, big, friendly, and extremely playful—just like Christopher and Nicholas.

Mrs. Donovan greets us, then herds her brood into the clinic. I follow behind Gran, with Sherlock close at my heels.

"Do they have an appointment?" I ask her under my breath.

Gran shakes her head. "No. I hope everything is all right."

"SHERLOCK!"

Christopher, Nicholas, Inky, and Shelby all pounce on my dog as soon as he puts a paw into the waiting room. Sherlock stands like a saint as Christopher pats his ears, Nicholas tosses him a ball, Inky smells his butt, and Shelby barks loudly, calling him to play. To the Donovans, Wild at Heart is not a veterinary clinic. It's where they come to play with Sherlock Holmes.

"What's the trouble today, Mrs. Donovan?" Gran shouts over the din.

Mrs. Donovan tries to keep an eye on her kids (all four of them) while she talks.

"I've got two of them, Dr. Mac," she starts. "Inky keeps biting his leg. The back one, on the right."

Sure enough, Inky pauses in mid-sniff to twist around quickly and nibble at his fur. Sometimes dogs use their teeth to scratch their itches. This spot looks like it's really bothering him. He's gnawing so hard that his dog tags are jingling. Maybe he has fleas.

"And this morning, Shelby did this," Mrs.

Donovan continues, holding out her left hand for Gran to inspect.

It is a perfectly normal left hand—no bites, scratches, or marks. It has a few freckles on it, but not as many as I have. Does her hand hurt? Does she think Gran will fix it? Maybe Mrs. Donovan has finally snapped from all the stress.

"Notice the missing wedding ring?" she says, her voice rising. "Shelby ate it. I'm a patient woman, Dr. Mac. I didn't complain when he ate my socks, or my bathing suit, or even part of the laundry room wall. But my wedding ring! How am I ever going to get it back?"

Gran's mouth twitches as she fights a smile. "It's OK. We'll get the ring. Dr. Gabe can X-ray Shelby while I check Inky's skin problem."

Mrs. Donovan clutches her purse. "Why do you have to X-ray?"

"I'd like to be safe. I want to make sure that the ring is there and that it isn't causing any kind of internal damage," Gran says. "As long as it isn't blocking anything, it should pop out Shelby's back end in a day or so. You'll just have to, ah, dig around a little whenever he has a bowel movement."

Mrs. Donovan's eyes widen. "You mean, look in his poops?" she says hoarsely.

Uh-oh. "Poop" is a magic word to three-year-olds, just like "underwear." The boys howl with laughter.

"Look in his poops?" Christopher shrieks.

"Look in his poops!" Nicholas replies.

Shelby and Inky bark excitedly, then jump on Sherlock, who looks at me, pleading for a rescue.

Mrs. Donovan swallows hard. "The X-ray sounds like a good idea. And perhaps Shelby could stay here. Until, you know . . ."

"Oh, I know," Gran assures her. "Until the ring 'appears.'"

✛

After some juggling, we all head to our assigned places. Dr. Gabe takes Shelby back to X-ray him, with Brenna and Sunita tagging along to make sure the dog doesn't eat any medical equipment. David has to leave to go school shopping with his mother. Mrs. Donovan agrees to stay in the waiting room with the boys while Gran and I check out Inky's leg. I let Sherlock escape into the kitchen, where Zoe can show him her new stapler. I'm sure he'll be thrilled.

Gran and I lead Inky into the Dolittle exam room, named for one of Gran's favorite fictional veterinarians. When she closes the door behind us, we both let out a sigh of relief.

"Nothing like a visit from the Donovans to make me appreciate how calm my life is," Gran says. "Now, let's take a look at our itchy patient."

I help Gran hoist Inky up onto the table. *Uff!* He's got to weigh at least forty pounds. The first time I saw him, he weighed two.

"He sure has grown," I say.

"He's what, six months old now?" Gran asks as she pets the overgrown pup and lets him smell her hands.

I flip open his medical chart. "Seven months."

"Time flies. You are an awfully big boy for seven months," Gran tells Inky. He flaps his tail from side to side, knocking the folder with his medical records to the floor.

Gran examines his eyes, ears, and mouth. Then she pets his head, neck, and chest, skillfully moving her hands over his fur. Animals can't tell us what's wrong with them, so vets are trained to carefully examine their bodies for clues.

At last, Gran steps back. "You're growing like a teenager, Inky. No wonder you and your brother eat everything in sight. Let's take a look at that leg."

I hold Inky's head while Gran gently examines

the area of wet fur where he's been licking and chewing. Inky flinches a bit. It must be sore.

"Bingo," Gran says. "A hot spot. Want to see?"

I crane my neck for a glimpse. Gran separates the fur so that I can see the hot spot. *Ouch.* It is twice as big as a quarter and a nasty red color. No wonder Inky's been itching it. Hot spots are little skin infections caused by bacteria. Once a dog starts working on them, they can get huge overnight.

Gran shaves the fur around the hot spot and cleans it with a special solution that will help dry the skin. She gives Inky a cortisone injection to soothe the itching.

"There." Gran studies her work. "I bet that feels better already. I'll send him home with some antibiotics to fight infection, and he'll be good to go!"

Inky lifts his right front paw.

"Look," I say. "He wants to shake and say thank you."

Gran takes his paw and shakes. "You're welcome, young man." She bends over and peers at his paw.

I know what's coming next. I open a drawer and take out a special pair of nail clippers that I hand to Gran.

Gran's eyebrows flash up in surprise. "How did you know that I wanted these?"

"I've only seen you do this a thousand times," I say.

Gran takes the clippers and spreads Inky's paw. "I guess this puppy isn't the only thing that's growing up," she says.

I smile to myself. Some people think Gran is a little gruff, but I know she's soft on the inside. She's just not a touchy-feely kind of person, which is fine with me.

I pet Inky while Gran trims his nails. You have to be careful with a dog's toenails. They actually have blood vessels in them, and if you trim back too far, it hurts the dog and the nails bleed. But Gran is a pro. In just a few minutes, all eighteen nails are trimmed without any trouble.

Gran sets Inky on the floor and tosses him a dog biscuit. He devours it in one gulp.

"Typical teenager," Gran chuckles. "Reminds me of you."

"I'm not a teenager yet," I say as I get out the broom and dustpan to sweep up the nail clippings. "I'm only twelve."

"You eat like one." Gran tosses another biscuit to Inky, who shakes with delight at the treat. "And you start middle school tomorrow."

"Don't remind me," I say.

Gran clips Inky's leash onto his collar. "You're going to love it."

I dump the clippings in the trash. "Is that why I feel like barfing whenever someone says 'middle school'?"

Gran looks over the tops of her bifocals at me. "You know the MacKenzie motto, my girl: 'No Fear.'"

Easy for her to say. Gran was an awesome student. She got scholarships to college and vet school because of her high-powered brain. I must take after the other side of the family.

Gran hugs Inky, and the dog gives her a slobbery kiss. "Don't worry, Maggie. It won't be as bad as you think."

THREE

Gran was right. Middle school is not as bad as I thought it would be.

It's worse.

My locker is two miles away from my classes, so I have to lug my books in a backpack all day. Each book feels like it weighs fifty pounds. I'm in real danger of tipping over backward.

All of my teachers give us homework. I have to read a chapter in social studies, write an essay for English, do fifty math problems, and make a poster for health. I'm never going to get through it all, not even if I work all weekend. I wish I could go home right now and never come back. Maybe I'll spend the afternoon begging Gran to let me go back to sixth grade.

But not yet. I have to suffer through one more class: science.

As soon as the bell rings, kids pour into the halls like streams flowing into a river. Since I'm shorter than everybody, I have to go with the flow, a small fish in the current of big bodies. I let the crowd carry me up the stairs and along the length of the building to the science wing.

Here it is, Room 222. "Mr. Carlson," it says in raised letters by the door.

I take a deep breath and cut across the fast-moving lanes of human traffic. I keep my elbows out and my head down, like I'm driving the lane to the basketball hoop.

Made it! I push open the door, and . . .

Wow!

There's a *dog* in here!

Not just any dog. This is a German shepherd, purebred by the looks of him. He's lying down next to the teacher's desk, his front paws elegantly crossed over each other. He looks full-grown. His coat is tan with a big black patch that wraps around his back. His ears are dark, but his tail is a golden color. He's wearing a funny harness around his chest with a square leather handle attached to the top of it. I've never seen one like that before.

As I step into the room, the dog's ears swivel. He looks me over quickly. His eyes are soft, brown, and intelligent. You know how some dogs look smarter than others? This guy looks like he could do all my homework tonight and still have time to play outside.

Am I going to walk past this magnificent creature and sit at an empty desk?

No way!

I crouch down and hold out a hand in friendship. He sniffs me quickly, picking up the smells of pencils, books, cafeteria hot dogs (blech, blech), and all the animals I take care of at home. He can probably smell my bad mood, too. He licks my hand once and smiles at me, his tail wagging happily.

I scratch him between his ears. "You sure are beautiful!" I say. "What are you doing in a place like this?"

"He's working," responds a kind voice.

I look up. Sitting behind the desk is a man. He's wearing a blue-and-white-checked shirt and a tie with a map of the solar system on it. I'm not great at guessing the age of grown-ups, but he's older than Dr. Gabe and a lot younger than Gran. He has blond hair, lighter than Zoe's, with a reddish beard and mustache.

"Please don't bother Scout," the man continues. "He needs to stay focused on his job."

"I was just petting him," I say. "I wasn't bothering him. He liked it."

The man smiles. "I understand. He loves the attention. But he's working right now. What's your name, please?"

Am I in trouble already? Can't be. I was just saying hello to this dog—to Scout. I lift my chin and look the man straight in the eye. "Maggie MacKenzie," I say clearly.

He shuffles through the papers on his desk, his fingertips skimming the surface.

"Margaret MacKenzie?" he asks.

"Not Margaret," I correct him. "Maggie."

"I'm Mr. Carlson, Maggie. Welcome to biology. If you take your seat, I'll explain all about Scout and his job."

This dog does not look like he's working. He's lying around, waiting for something fun to happen. Mr. Carlson is busy collecting some papers, so I sneak in one more pat on Scout's head before I stand up.

"What is his job, exactly?" I ask.

Mr. Carlson puts the papers down. "He's a guide dog," he answers. "My guide dog." He looks up at me. "I'm blind."

✚

Blind? How can a teacher be blind? I'm still in a daze as I take my seat. Did he say just what I thought he said?

The other kids in the class are all exchanging glances. They look just as confused as I am. Scout watches the door as the last stragglers hurry in. His ears perk up as the bell rings. It's time for class to begin.

The science classroom is like the other rooms I've seen today, longer than it is wide, the far wall filled with windows. What sets it apart is the collection of cages crowded on the broad counter below the windows. The cages contain all kinds of small animals: mice, gerbils, hamsters, guinea pigs, and a large rabbit. As the rabbit hops from one end of its cage to the other, Scout watches it eagerly. I wonder what he's thinking.

Mr. Carlson stands up and walks around to the front of his desk, his fingertips gently brushing against the side of it. He looks out over the classroom. No, wait. He can't be looking, can he?

Scout starts to stand up, his eyes on his companion. He looks anxious, as if he's waiting for a command. But he doesn't get one. Mr. Carlson leans against the front of the desk and crosses his arms over his chest. Scout makes a small whining noise, but he lies back down and rests his head on his front paws.

"As you might have guessed, I'm your teacher, Mr. Carlson, and this is seventh-grade science—biology. Biology is the cool science, the study of living things. We're going to study cells, body parts, worms, rats . . . you're going to love it."

I already do! A class with a dog? I'm in heaven—well, as close to heaven as you can get in school.

Mr. Carlson continues. "I've taught seventh-grade science for ten years. Middle-school students are the best. You're energetic, you're curious, and you tie your shoes by yourselves."

That gets a few giggles. Mr. Carlson smiles and relaxes a little.

"Now, let me talk about the whole blindness thing."

The giggles stop.

"Two years ago, I developed a condition called retinitis pigmentosa. Most people call it RP. RP made me blind. I can't see you."

"I took last year off from teaching and went to a special school. I learned how to read Braille, a code that uses raised dots, and lots of other things that help me get around. It was hard, but I made it. Today is my first day back in the classroom."

He stops and takes a deep breath. The class is silent.

"I am a teacher who is blind, a very good teacher. I'll use my computer a lot. It has a special program on it that reads text out loud. Anything you can read on a computer screen, I can hear. Some-times I'll ask you to help me by writing on the blackboard. And if anyone is planning to cheat—don't. I'm blind, not stupid."

The class groans a bit. Mr. Carlson smiles.

"Now, a few class rules. Don't raise your hand. I won't call on you."

A couple of kids laugh at that.

"If you have a question, just ask—quietly, not at the top of your lungs. My ears work fine. I'll hold a meeting for parents next week. I suspect your folks are going to have a few questions.

"Going blind has meant a lot of changes for me. Let me introduce you to the newest one. Scout, come."

Scout springs into action, happy to be doing something. He trots over to Mr. Carlson and sits at his feet.

"Scout is my guide dog."

The dog looks up at the sound of his name, his mouth open and tongue hanging out. He is so sweet!

"When I have to walk somewhere, Scout acts as my eyes. I give him a direction, like forward, left, or right, and Scout walks that way. His most important job is to keep me safe. He guides me around things, like chairs that aren't pushed in or garbage cans on a sidewalk."

Mr. Carlson leans over and picks up the handle attached to Scout's harness. Scout stands up. He's ready to go to work.

"When this harness is on, Scout is working. Do not call his name, pet him, whistle, throw things, bark, meow—nothing. If he is distracted, he can't do his job properly."

Darn. What's the point of having a dog in the room if we have to ignore him?

"Scout, forward."

With his head up high and eyes ahead, Scout leads Mr. Carlson down the center aisle. In the middle of the room, Mr. Carlson says, "Scout, right," and the dog turns to the right. Mr. Carlson hesitates, feeling the air with his hand, then turns right.

"What do you do in the halls?" I ask. "They're hard enough to walk in even if you can see."

The class laughs, and Mr. Carlson smiles. "Who's speaking?" he asks.

"Me. Maggie MacKenzie."

"Let's just say the halls are a challenge, Maggie. Scout, forward."

Scout leads Mr. Carlson forward a few more steps, then stops. They have reached the edge of the room and are standing in front of the counter that runs below the windows.

"Go on, Scout," Mr. Carlson instructs. "Forward."

Scout tilts his head to one side. He's confused. If he keeps walking, Mr. Carlson is going to run right into the counter.

"You can't go any farther," I say. "You're at the edge of the room."

Mr. Carlson reaches out and knocks his hand on the mice cage. "Oh. Thanks. I guess that's what Scout was trying to say, too." His face gets a little red. I think he's embarrassed. I can tell Scout and Mr. Carlson haven't been working together for very long.

"What are all the animals for?" I ask.

"Meet Carlson's Critters." He places his hand on top of the mice cage. "I grew up with small pets like these. We lived in an apartment, and we weren't allowed to have dogs or cats. I loved these little guys. I almost got thrown out of seventh grade for bringing a gerbil to school in my shirt pocket."

I think he's my dream teacher.

Scout's nose quivers as he smells the rodents, but he doesn't move. I'm impressed. Most of the dogs I know would have jumped up, put their paws on the counter, and knocked over a cage by now.

"I'm looking for a volunteer," Mr. Carlson says. "I need someone to clean out these cages and help with the critters."

My hand shoots up in the air. Scout looks at me and tilts his head to the side.

"If nobody is interested, the janitors said they would keep doing it, but I think it might be fun . . ."

I wave my whole arm. I was born to do this—*pick me! Pick me!*

Then it hits me. *Oh, duh. Oh, double duh-duh.* He can't see my hand. He can't see me.

"I'll do it!" I shout.

Scout smiles and wags his tail with excitement.

"Let me guess," Mr. Carlson says. "Maggie MacKenzie. Excellent. That takes care of the introduction. I need someone to pass out the textbooks that are on my desk. We are going to start the year with a quick review of the human body. Open to chapter six, and get out your notebooks. Our first unit is 'The Eye.'"

FOUR

Even though Mr. Carlson makes us take pages of notes and gives us way too much homework, I'm happy when I walk out of his classroom. He said I could take care of his "critters" with my friends from Wild at Heart. Once he sees the great job we do, I know he'll let me play with Scout. I still can't believe I have a dog in my science class!

The bus ride home is loud and long. Everyone talks at the same time. All of my friends have stories to tell and big plans for the rest of the year. Zoe wants to run for student council, David is trying out for the play, and Brenna is planning on joining the school newspaper as a photographer. Even Sunita is happy. She remembered her combination and finished half of her homework in study hall.

"Lucky you," Brenna says. "I'm going to be doing homework all weekend."

Homework.

A familiar feeling rumbles in my stomach. Every block in my agenda book is filled with homework assignments. I'm in the same boat as Brenna.

I'll think about it later.

When I get home, I head straight for the Dolittle Room, where Gran is examining a two-foot-long green iguana.

"I'm back!" I announce, dumping my backpack in the corner.

Gran and the iguana look up at the sound of the pack hitting the floor. "You survived," Gran says. "Good."

"Just barely." I crouch down for a better look at the iguana. He sticks his tongue out at me. "Guess what? My science teacher has a guide dog. He's blind. My teacher, I mean, not the dog. Scout's a German shepherd. He's the smartest, best-looking dog I have ever seen."

"You'd better not let Sherlock hear you talk like that," Gran kids. She takes a small light and shines it in the eyes of the iguana. The iguana blinks. "What's your teacher like?"

I sit on the floor and loosen the laces of my sneakers. "Mr. Carlson seems great, but his class is a lot of work. My hand still hurts from all the notes we had to take. He must have just started working with Scout. I don't think they've gotten the hang of working together yet. I tried to pet Scout, but Mr. Carlson stopped me."

Gran picks up the iguana and gently feels his limbs. "You should never touch a working guide dog. That's common sense and good manners. Has Mr. Carlson ever had a dog before?"

I shake my head. "Never. He likes rats."

"Rats?"

"OK, not rats. Mice, gerbils, hamsters, rabbits. Carlson's Critters, he calls them. The science room is loaded with them. I signed up to help take care of them. Brenna and the others are going to help, too."

Gran nods. "That's sensible. You're the most qualified kids in the whole school. I'm glad you volunteered."

"Umm . . ." I hesitate as I pull off my sneakers. "I sort of volunteered you, too. Some of the critters could use a checkup."

Gran puts the iguana on the exam table and watches it closely as it walks to the end. She scoops it up before it leaps off. "I'd be happy to look at them. Now, tell me—how was the rest of school?"

"Except for Scout?" I take my socks off and stuff them in my sneakers. I wiggle my toes in the cool air. *Aaaah.* "School stinks. The halls are crowded, my locker is miles away from my classes, and my teachers are crazy. They gave me a ton of homework!"

Gran pretends that she's shocked. "A ton? Two thousand pounds of homework? How cruel! I'll complain to the principal at once." She fights to keep a smile off her face.

I roll my eyes. She's being sarcastic. Is there anything worse than a grown-up making jokes about homework?

"Seriously, Gran. I have so much to do it's not funny. Mr. Carlson is the worst. He told us to copy our notes from class *and* read a whole chapter *and* study a list of vocab words. It's going to take forever." I lean against the wall and cross my arms over my chest. "He wants us to review our class notes every night!"

Gran takes off her glasses and lets them dangle from their beaded chain. "You can handle it. A little bit of work never hurt anyone. And your study skills got a lot better after working with the tutor."

Oh, blah, blah, blah. I hate it when people pretend that homework is not a big deal. You'd think that Gran would understand. We had a huge blow-up about my grades last year, and that was when she brought in the tutor. I can tell we're going to have more blowups this year. Maybe we should fireproof the walls of the clinic.

Gran is winding up for another lecture on how "homework prepares you for the classroom" and "it never killed anyone" and "a bad attitude just makes things worse." I've got to divert her.

I force a cheerful look on my face and point to the iguana. "So, what's wrong with this guy?"

Gran pauses, studying me. She has raised me since I was a tiny baby. She knows me better than anyone in the world. She can tell I'm dodging. But she nods once. The school lecture is on hold, for a few minutes at least.

"This is Iggy," Gran says as she picks up her patient. "He's suffering from a very bad diet. Feel gently along his spine. Notice the bumps?"

I cross the room and lightly run my fingertips along Iggy's back. Iggy turns his head to watch what I'm doing. The end of his tail flicks nervously back and forth. His back feels funny, like there are little peas under his skin.

"What's wrong with him?" I ask.

"Metabolic bone disease," Gran says. "His owners have been feeding him cat food."

"Let me guess. Cat food is bad for iguanas."

"You got it. He needs lots of fresh greens, with some veggies and fruit every once in a while. Iggy's bones are weak and spongy. They're close to breaking. He needs a total change in diet."

She gently moves her green patient to a small cage. There is a pile of crisp leaves in a bowl for him. Iggy sniffs the leaves suspiciously, then turns up his nose.

"Isn't he going to eat them?" I ask.

"He thinks cat food tastes better. It's what he's used to," Gran says as she washes her hands briskly with hot water and soap. "Changes are hard. I'm sure you'd agree. Now . . ." she starts, turning her full attention on me.

Gran has blue eyes. When she wants to (like now), she can make them like lasers, pinning her helpless victim against the wall.

Here it comes.

"The halls are crowded, the teachers are crazy, and you have a 'ton' of homework," she says. "Since you have so much of it, you should get started right away, don't you think?"

We're interrupted by the jangling sound of the bell over the front door. The next patient has arrived.

I open the door.

I don't believe it—it's Scout! He's sitting next to Mr. Carlson in the middle of the waiting room, holding up his right front paw. The fur is stained with blood. Mr. Carlson turns toward us.

"We need the vet right away."

FIVE

"What happened, Mr. Carlson?" I ask anxiously as Gran lifts Scout onto the exam table.

"I'm sorry," Mr. Carlson says. "Who is speaking?"

"It's me, Maggie MacKenzie, from eighth-period biology. Is Scout OK? Is his foot broken?"

Gran holds up her hand. "He just got here, Maggie. Give me a few minutes."

"Maggie? What are you doing here?" Mr. Carlson asks, puzzled until he makes the connection. "Ahh, Dr. Mac—MacKenzie!" he says. "You're related?"

Gran scratches Scout between the ears. "Maggie is my granddaughter. She lives with me and helps out at the clinic."

My teacher nods. "You told me about that at the end of class, didn't you?"

I start to nod, then say, "Yes. What happened to Scout?"

37

Mr. Carlson takes a deep breath and quietly explains. "I stepped on his paw. We were running late because we got lost. When I realized what time it was, I rushed and landed right on Scout's paw with my boot."

I glance at his feet. Mr. Carlson wears fancy cowboy boots. I didn't notice that in class. They are pretty neat looking, but I can see how their thick heels could have hurt a paw.

While Mr. Carlson's talking, Gran quickly examines the dog's eyes and mouth and takes his pulse. She always checks an animal's overall health before she zeroes in on what is bothering him. Scout watches Gran, but he keeps one eye on Mr. Carlson, too. I think the guide dog looks a little anxious. Maybe he thinks he messed up.

"I could tell he was limping right away," Mr. Carlson continues, "and I felt the blood on his paw. I called a taxi and told the driver to bring me to the best vet in town. She brought me here." He rubs his forehead. "I hope his foot's not broken."

Gran slips on a pair of latex gloves. "Let's not jump to conclusions before we have all the facts. Scout can put weight on the paw, which is a good sign. I'm going to take a closer look now. Mr. Carlson, would you please ask Scout to lie down?"

"Scout, down," Mr. Carlson commands.

Scout obeys right away, stretching until he is lying down perfectly. He looks at Mr. Carlson expectantly. He's waiting for praise. You should always congratulate a dog when he's done the right thing.

Mr. Carlson is silent.

"Good boy, Scout," I say loudly. I reach over and pet his head, and he pants happily. "He listened to you perfectly, Mr. Carlson," I say.

"The guide-dog school trained him very well," Mr. Carlson says.

Scout looks at his human companion, eagerly waiting for something, anything, but Mr. Carlson doesn't move toward him.

Gran looks at me and gives a little shake of her head. She's thinking the same thing I am, but now is not the time to mention it.

"Want me to hold his head?" I ask.

"Sure," Gran says. She gently touches Scout's left paw, watching him closely.

"Isn't it his right paw that's hurt?" I ask Gran.

"It is," Gran says, squeezing the left paw a little. "Some dogs don't like their paws touched at all. I'm starting with his good one to see if he is comfortable with it."

Scout looks relaxed. He lets Gran feel his good paw without any complaint.

"Good boy," Gran says as she gives him a friendly pat. "Now let's see the other one."

She picks up the injured paw and cradles it carefully in her hand. Scout watches her, but he isn't showing any signs of pain.

"Maggie, get me an antiseptic wash and some gauze pads. I need to clean off this blood."

I quickly hand the big bottle to Gran, and she gently sprays antiseptic over Scout's paw. I get a handful of paper towels ready to sop up the mess.

"That's better," Gran says. She bends over to see the pads of the paw. When she touches his right paw, Scout whimpers and tries to pull it out of her hands.

"Shh, shh," I say softly. I stroke the fur on his neck and shoulder. "I know it hurts," I say, "but it's just for a minute. Then she'll make it feel better. It's OK, Scout. You're a good dog."

I look over at Mr. Carlson. He can't see any of this. I close my eyes to imagine what it's like for him. I can hear Scout panting, Brenna talking out in the waiting room, a radio playing down the hall. Scout whimpers again, and I open my eyes.

"How does it look?" Mr. Carlson asks.

"Not too bad," Gran answers. "We washed the blood off. He has a cut on the side of the pads. The boot pinched it. His nails are in good shape—none of them are split or broken. That's really good. It can be very painful for a dog to lose a toenail. Right now I'm feeling his metacarpals, the little bones in his foot. His foot pads are a little swollen and tender, especially around the cut, but I don't think anything is broken."

After working her fingers along the bones in his paw, ankle, and foreleg, Gran gently flexes Scout's foot. Scout doesn't flinch.

"Ah, you're fine," Gran tells him. "Do you want to feel, Mr. Carlson?"

"Yes, thank you," my teacher says. He steps closer to the exam table.

"Let me show you on his good leg," Gran suggests. She takes Mr. Carlson's right hand and sets it on Scout's left leg. Scout wags his tail and leans against Mr. Carlson's arm.

Gran plows ahead. "Can you feel how thick the skin is on his pads?" Gran asks as she guides Mr. Carlson's fingers to the bottom of Scout's paw. "It is kind of like a moccasin—thick enough to protect, but sensitive. It *is* bruised, but it will heal. Scout's bones are fine. He has a compression injury along with a contusion."

"Meaning my boot squashed his paw and cut it," Mr. Carlson adds with a wince.

"Exactly," Gran says. "But don't be too hard on yourself. These things happen to everyone."

"How long will it take Scout to recover? Should he rest? Can he walk with me?"

"It's not that bad," Gran says with a friendly laugh. "I'll bandage his paw, but he can walk fine. He can still guide you. The skin will heal quickly. I'll give you some antibiotic ointment to use."

Mr. Carlson frowns. "The bandage will need changing, won't it?"

"I could change the bandage for you," I say. "After class. Or Gran can show you how to do it."

Gran rips open a package of sterile pads. "Come close and put your hands on mine as I wrap the bandage. Then you can try it on your own."

Mr. Carlson thinks about it for a minute, then nods his head once. "That might work."

Gran wraps the injured paw with Mr. Carlson following every step. "Maggie tells me that you and Scout are new partners," she says. "How long have you been working together?"

"Exactly one week. We're going back to the guide-dog school tomorrow for a follow-up visit. It's a good thing, too. I have lots of questions."

"Scout looks like a skilled guide," Gran says. "I'm sure the two of you make a terrific team."

Scout wags his tail happily. He can tell when someone gives him a compliment.

"We're still learning," Mr. Carlson says. "I wish we had had more time to get used to each other before I went back to teaching. There's just so much going on right now with school starting: my students, my dog, not getting lost in the building . . ."

"Didn't they teach you about all this stuff at the guide-dog school?" I ask.

"They did a great job," Mr. Carlson says. "But it's still a big adjustment."

Gran tapes the bandage in place. "I've read about guide-dog training, but I've never seen the school. Do you want some company tomorrow?"

"That would be great," Mr. Carlson says. "In fact, I'd feel better if you came along. You can explain what happened to the school's veterinarian."

They discuss the details of getting together on Saturday while I put away the bandaging supplies. After breakfast, Gran will pick up Mr. Carlson and Scout and drive to the guide-dog school in her van.

"Would you like to come, too, Maggie?" Mr. Carlson asks as Gran helps Scout off the table.

Spend Saturday with Scout?

Scout shakes his coat once and looks up at me. "Sure!"

Scout grins and wags his tail.

"Good. That's settled," Mr. Carlson says as he bends to pick up Scout's leash. "You're sure it won't hurt his foot to guide me?"

"Scout's honor," Gran says, with a chuckle.

Mr. Carlson grins. "That's a good one, Dr. Mac."

Scout whines just a tiny bit and scootches closer to Mr. Carlson. He looks up at his companion, waiting. Why doesn't Mr. Carlson pet Scout? That little whine was Scout's way of asking for attention. Maybe my teacher's not much of a dog person.

"Why don't you give him a hug," Gran suggests. "I think Scout could use some reassurance."

Mr. Carlson pats Scout's head. "That's the kind of thing I have trouble remembering," he admits. "I still feel awkward around him. Between teaching again and getting used to Scout, my brain is ready to explode. I feel like a kid—a kid with too much homework and a pop quiz every day."

I know exactly what that feels like.

SIX

This is torture.

I am locked in a speeding van with my grandmother and my biology teacher, who spend the two-hour drive to the guide-dog school yakking about mice and frogs and microscopes. I wish someone would develop one of those sci-fi transporters. We'd be with the dogs in no time!

Scout sleeps by Mr. Carlson's feet. I thought maybe he could sit next to me, but Gran said no. I think she wants Scout to be as close to Mr. Carlson as possible, to help them bond. I don't know why Mr. Carlson didn't click with Scout right away. Maybe it's because he never had a dog before. I just hope it doesn't hurt Scout's feelings. Even working dogs need a little TLC—tender loving care.

The guide-dog school is on the edge of a busy town called Franklin. The school reminds me of a

college campus, with low brick buildings and walking paths that wind around beautiful gardens. As
we park in the visitors' lot, we see a small group
of blind people with their dogs and instructors
walking down the sidewalk toward town.

I sit up straighter. The guide dogs are gorgeous:
they're golden retrievers, black Labs, and German
shepherds. They walk quickly with their heads up,
tongues lolling out of their mouths, and tails wagging eagerly. An entire school devoted to people
and dogs—sign me up!

Before Mr. Carlson takes Gran to the veterinary
center, he introduces me to John Liu. John was his
instructor. He trained Scout and taught Mr. Carlson
how to work with the dog.

John (he says I have to call him that) has short
black hair and is wearing jeans, a dark green polo
shirt, hiking boots, and a faded Mets baseball cap. He
looks more like a mountain climber than a teacher.

"Pleased to meet you," I say as I shake his hand.
Gran is big on hand shaking.

"Pleasure to meet you, too," he says.

"We thought you might be able to show Maggie
around," Mr. Carlson says.

"I'd love to," John answers.

We agree to meet at the van later. Gran, Mr.

Carlson, and Scout leave to visit the school's clinic. John turns to me.

"Now, Maggie, I could give you a tour of the grounds, complete with video presentation and an armful of brochures."

Oh, no. That sounds like a class trip to the Museum of Boring Things. I want to see dogs!

He pushes up the brim of his cap. "But I remember what it felt like to be a kid," he continues. "Follow me."

✚

We walk down a grassy hill to a long building that has dog runs jutting out one side. I hear barking. My heart starts to beat faster.

We step through the door of the building and—wow!—a litter of German shepherd puppies! They look to be about four weeks old, chasing, tumbling, and playing in a giant puppy pen. The mom dog is napping in the corner. She lifts her head to look at the intruders and wags her tail happily when she sees John.

"They are so cute!" I squeal. I'm normally not the kind of person who squeals, but puppies bring out my inner Zoe.

"Will the mom let me pet them?" New mothers

can be very protective of their puppies.

"Sure," John says as he scratches the mom dog's ears. "We want the dogs to be as sociable as possible. She is very comfortable with visitors."

I step into the puppy pen and kneel down. The puppies are all over me in an instant, kissing my face, licking my hands and arms, jumping up and down. I burst into giggles. Their ears are still floppy, and their fur is more like fuzz. When they grow up, they will be regal, dignified dogs like Scout. Right now, they are tubby little fluff-balls that want to chew on my hair. It's great.

Every school in America should have a puppy pen. That way any kid having a bad day could visit for fifteen minutes of puppy love. That would cure anyone's bad mood. I bet grades would go up, too.

"Do you raise all the puppies here?" I ask as I toss a ball across the pen.

John takes a brush from a hook on the wall and starts to groom the mom dog's coat. She closes her eyes in pleasure.

"We breed all our dogs here," he explains. "The pups stay with their mother for eight weeks. Then we send them out to volunteer puppy-raising families. The puppy raisers take care of their pups until they're about eighteen months old. They teach them basic obedience and make sure that they're exposed to lots of social experiences."

"Do they teach any of the commands that the blind people use?" I ask.

"Only basic obedience, like 'Sit,' 'Stay,' and 'Come.' The real work starts when the dogs come back here. If they pass their medical exams, the dogs are assigned an instructor, like me. We work with the dogs for about four months, teaching them the skills they need to be successful guide dogs. When the companions arrive at the school, they work with their dogs for a month. Assuming all goes well, the dogs and companions graduate and leave as a team."

"Wow," I say. "That's a lot of change, a lot of moving around for the dogs. How can they bond with anyone?"

John picks up the tufts of fur from the floor. "They are totally surrounded by love and affection every step of the way. Big changes are easier to handle if you know people love you—that's true for dogs and people. But it takes time and patience. The tricky part is when the dog and blind companion leave here and go back to real life. The outside world takes some getting used to."

"I think that's what Mr. Carlson and Scout are

going through," I say.

"What do you mean?" John asks.

I stroke the head of the sleepy puppy in my lap and explain what I know. John lifts his cap, scratches the back of his head, and puts the cap back on.

"I knew it would be a challenge, starting with Scout and then going back to teaching right away," he says. "But James, Mr. Carlson, is a really independent guy. And Scout is a smart dog, well suited for a teacher. They need time together, and they need to keep up on their training. And James has to remember to be affectionate with Scout."

The puppy in my lap lets out a little snore. I wonder if there is something I can do to help. Teach my teacher? Is that possible?

"Come on," John says. "You've seen the puppies. Now I want to show you how we train the adult dogs."

✚

"This is Nugent," John says as he opens a kennel door. A medium-sized golden retriever with a shiny reddish coat bounds out. John bends down and hugs him, ruffling his fur.

"Do you want to pet him?" he asks.

"Can I?" I ask, puzzled. "Gran told me I shouldn't

pet a guide dog, not even a little."

John hooks a leash on Nugent's collar. "She's right. But Nugent isn't wearing his guide harness right now, so he's off duty. He knows that he's not working."

I kneel in front of the happy dog and let him smell my hand. He sniffs it over very carefully, then gives it a big slurp.

"I like you, too," I chuckle. As I reach out to pet him, Nugent rolls over so that I can scratch his belly. Oooh, he loves that!

After a few minutes of petting and playing, John fastens on Nugent's harness. It looks exactly like Scout's. Nugent stops acting goofy as soon as the harness is on. He sits attentively by John's left foot.

"Do you want to walk with him?" John asks.

"Can I? Wow! Sure!"

I take the harness from John. Nugent looks over his shoulder and smiles at me. John tells me to grip the handle lightly and to keep it back by my left leg.

"He's there to guide you, not to drag you down the street. But be prepared. Nugent walks quickly. The commands are simple: 'Forward,' 'Halt,' 'Left,' 'Right.' If he slows down to investigate or smell something, you say, 'Hup-up.' Got it?"

"Got it," I say. "Nugent, forward."

And we're off—fast! I have to power-walk to keep up with him.

"You weren't kidding," I tell John. "What happens if Nugent gets a handler with short legs, like me?"

John strides beside us easily. "Matching the dog and handler is the most important thing we do. Nugent will be a good guide for a tall, athletic person, someone with a strong personality, who isn't afraid to charge into a crowd. Relax your hand a bit."

Good advice. I'm clutching the handle way too tightly.

"We'll walk through the park to town. When we get all the way down to the corner, tell Nugent to take a right," John instructs.

We walk along in silence for a few minutes, enjoying the beautiful day and the company of a good dog. My legs have warmed up, and I can match Nugent's gait now. This is different from walking Sherlock Holmes. Sherlock (and every other dog I've walked) wants to hunt around, smell, and explore. Nugent wants to move, to get where we're going.

Scattered around the park are other guide dogs working with instructors or their new handlers. I think I see Mr. Carlson and Scout, but I don't want to holler and distract them. The only sounds are good ones—people praising dogs, telling them how good and wonderful they are. This place has what Brenna would call "good vibes."

"Can I close my eyes?" I ask. "You know . . ."

John nods. "You want to see what it feels like for James and Scout, right? Go right ahead. Trust the dog. He knows how to take care of you."

I look straight ahead. The sidewalk is smooth. There's nothing in our way. I close my eyes and keep walking.

"Wow! It feels like we're speeding up." I open my eyes. "It's kind of scary."

"Try it again," John urges.

I squeeze my eyes shut. I'm not going to open them again. I'd like to slow down, but Nugent is setting the pace. The harness! With my eyes shut, I notice the position of the harness in my hand a lot more. I can feel how Nugent walks, his shoulders rolling slightly from side to side.

"Wait a minute," I say, my eyes still closed. "What's he doing?"

Nugent has slowed down. Now he stops, still standing at my left side.

"What's wrong?" I ask.

"Nothing. He's waiting for you to tell him what to do," John says. "The sidewalk here is shaped like a T. You can go left or right. If you keep going straight, you'll walk into the road. Nugent is trained to cross only at corners, so he won't let you do that."

"OK, Nugent, right."

The handle shifts as Nugent turns to the right. I step to the right, and we are off again.

"Great job, Maggie," John says. "Tell him to halt, and I'll take over."

"Nugent, halt." The dog responds perfectly, and I open my eyes. "Good boy!" I say. He wags his tail and smiles.

John takes the handle of the harness from me. "You're really good at picking up Nugent's signals," he says. He takes a thick blindfold from his back pocket and ties it so that his eyes are completely covered. "Forward, Nugent."

We start walking again.

"Don't you have to tell him where you want to go, like, 'Nugent, let's get a water ice,' or 'Nugent, take me to the grocery store'?" I ask.

"Nope, that's a common myth," John says. "Guide dogs don't take you places. They follow directions. It is up to the handler to know where she's going. Think of it this way: the handler is the navigator and the dog is the driver. Nugent, left."

Nugent guides John to a branch of the sidewalk that goes off to the left.

"Traffic lights are another myth," John continues. "Some people think that guide dogs know it is safe to cross the street when the light changes from green to red. That's wrong. Dogs don't watch the light. They watch for cars and listen to the commands of their handler."

As John talks, I keep an eye on Nugent. We pass a bakery, a flower shop, and a deli that smells like cheese steak sandwiches, but nothing distracts him. He walks right past a woman leading two yipping Maltese dogs without a glance. He doesn't even sniff a fire hydrant. It's amazing.

"Good boy, Nugent!" John praises enthusiastically. Nugent wags his tail and keeps walking.

"We're coming up to a busy intersection," I warn.

"I know," John says. "Nugent knows, too. Just watch. Whatever you do, don't grab the harness. That's like grabbing the steering wheel of a car. It will ruin his confidence."

Nugent stops at the corner. The traffic rushes past us on the street. Then the light changes.

"I listen carefully to make sure that the traffic has

stopped, and then we go," John explains. "Nugent, forward."

As John steps off the curb, a car comes around the corner, right in his path. Before I can say anything, Nugent freezes, and John hastily steps back on the curb. The car drives past us.

"Good boy," John says, giving Nugent a hug. "Now forward."

Nugent checks the road, then leads John safely across. I walk with them.

"That was incredible," I say when we reach the other side. "He saw that car coming and stopped you. He saved your life!"

"That's what we call intelligent disobedience," John says. "It is the hardest thing to teach. The dog has to disobey a command from the handler when he knows the handler might be hurt. Guide dogs do that every day."

We cross another street and head back toward the school.

"I don't want you to get the wrong impression, Maggie," John says. "Guide dogs are not super-heroes or robots. They are just highly trained dogs that work with motivated, independent blind people."

Just like my science teacher.

✚

John and Nugent drop me off at the van. I find Gran still at the vet center deep in a discussion about hip problems. She can talk about hip problems for hours. I wander around until I find Mr. Carlson sitting on a bench under an ancient maple tree. Mr. Carlson has a Braille magazine in his lap, but he's not reading it. Scout rests at his feet, staring at the guide dogs and their handlers still practicing in the park.

I walk over to the maple tree and sit down. "Hey, Mr. Carlson," I say.

"Hi, Maggie," he says. "Did you have fun?"

"You'd better believe it." I tell him all about the puppies and my walk with Nugent. He doesn't say much, like his mind is somewhere else.

"How is Scout?" I ask. "Did the vet agree with Gran?"

Mr. Carlson nods. "Yep. The swelling of his paw has already gone down a bit. He's fine."

"That's good," I say.

"Um-hmm," he replies.

What do I say now? I can't just leave. That would be rude. I think about it for a minute.

"What did you mean yesterday when you said that you and Scout got lost?"

"Oh, that." Mr. Carlson gives a little laugh. "It

would have been funny if it wasn't so awful. I didn't think I would have any trouble finding my way around the school. I taught there, sighted, for ten years."

"And?"

"And I couldn't find the upstairs conference room. Talk about embarrassing! I felt like an idiot."

I don't say anything.

Mr. Carlson continues. "And then the way I stepped on Scout's paw and hurt him . . . well, it wasn't a very good way to end the first day of school. Coming back here," he waves his arm to show the campus of the guide-dog school, "makes me realize how much I'm doing wrong."

I lean forward and put my elbows on my knees. He sounds serious. Scout turns around to look. I bet he can hear the defeated tone in his companion's voice. I wish I could pet him and tell him it will be all right.

"It can't be that bad," I say.

"You don't know the half of it," he says. "I'm too busy for Scout's obedience lessons. He was upset when we got lost. He thought it was his fault, but it was mine. I wonder . . ."

"Wonder what?"

He takes a deep breath. "I wonder if I should

have waited a year—gotten back into the swing of teaching, *then* applied for a guide dog." He pauses and smooths his beard. "I wonder if I should give him back."

"You can't!" I exclaim. "You can't give up! I know about dogs, Mr. Carlson. Scout is amazing. He's like a genius dog, I swear. He wants to work with you. You just need more time together."

"That's what they all say."

"I know you think I'm just a kid, but I really do know dogs. You just have to . . ."

I stop. Who am I to tell a teacher what to do?

"No, go on," he says. "What were you going to say?"

Gulp. Go ahead, MacKenzie.

"First, you have to tell Scout when he does a good job. Praise him. If you don't, he thinks he messed up. It's like if you gave us a test, then never told us what our grades were. That wouldn't teach us very much, would it?"

Mr. Carlson feels along the bench until he finds Scout's long leash. He holds it loosely in his hands. "I hadn't thought about it like that before."

Scout sits up.

"Pet him. Give him a hug," I suggest. "He knows something is bothering you. He wants to help. He wants to make you happy and proud."

Mr. Carlson gingerly puts his hand out. Scout leans into it. Mr. Carlson pats his dog once, then puts his hand on the bench.

"You're being very helpful, Maggie, but I don't think you're old enough to understand how complicated this is. I want the best for Scout. That's why I think that maybe he should go to someone else. I'm not ready for him."

The stubborn part of me flares up. "You're going to quit?" I ask angrily. "Don't you believe in that stuff that teachers always tell kids: 'Try your best,' 'You can do it,' 'Don't give up'? Is it all a lie?"

Scout looks at me anxiously, his tail turned in, his head lowered a bit in a submissive posture.

"Sorry, Scout," I apologize. "I'm not mad at you. Mr. Carlson, you have to give yourself a chance. Working with Scout, obedience training, learning to love and respect each other—that's homework. You're the king of giving out homework. It's your turn to *do* some. Don't give up. It's too important."

"It sounds like you've heard this before," he remarks.

I kick at a tuft of grass. "Yeah, you could say that. I've heard it a lot."

We sit quietly for a moment. The guide dogs and handlers are walking back from town. The park is quiet except for the calls of mockingbirds and blue jays. Mr. Carlson strokes his beard for a while, then speaks.

"How long should I give it?" he asks.

"What do you mean?"

"You're the dog expert," he says. "How long should I try? A month? Two months?"

"A week," I blurt out.

"A week?"

"That's all you need. Think about it. He's a trained guide dog. You are—"

"A trained blind guy?" he interrupts with a sly grin.

"You know what I mean. You know the basics, but you have some work to do. And I can help. I've worked with lots of dogs and their owners. I could watch you work with Scout—give you some tips."

Mr. Carlson laughs, a real belly laugh. "Tips would be helpful, but you know what I really need? Someone to help me map out the middle school so that we don't get lost again."

"I can do that, I think. I got lost the first day, too. Maybe we should learn our way around together."

"Can you meet me before school on Monday?"

"Will you spend the rest of the weekend telling Scout he's awesome and smart and wonderful?"

Mr. Carlson nods. "I promise. It sounds like we have a deal." He puts out his hand to shake.

I grasp his hand and shake once.

"Deal!"

SEVEN

Sunday goes by in a blur because Gran goes into a rare fit of housecleaning. Zoe and I pick up, scrub, dust, vacuum, pick up some more, try to watch TV, get kicked out of the family room, start the laundry, and mop the kitchen floor.

I'm actually grateful when Gran says it's time to do homework. But, man, am I tired!

OK, get a grip. It's time to be Middle-School Maggie, ready to take on the scariest homework assignment in the world. I spread out my agenda book, folders, and binder and line up my pens and pencils like toy soldiers.

Attack!

I read my social studies chapter (the Constitution—takes forever), write my English essay (well, OK, it's the sloppy copy), and finish fifty math problems (argh!). I take a quick break to let out

Sherlock, then sit back down to do my biology.

I am supposed to memorize my notes. How do you do that? And we have to know the whole chapter about the eye *and* the vocabulary words? Mr. Carlson's nuts. No one could expect that much out of a group of seventh-graders.

I read the chapter and vocab words. Once.

There, I did it. I studied.

I hope Mr. Carlson and Scout did their homework, too.

✚

Gran drops me off at school early on Monday morning. I sit on the front steps, watching the teachers pull into the parking lot. How is Mr. Carlson going to get here?

Here comes the answer—a bus. It drops him off at the corner in front of the building. The traffic is thick with rush-hour commuters. Mr. Carlson and Scout wait until the light changes, then cross the street safely.

"I'm over here," I call. "On the steps."

"Forward, Scout," Mr. Carlson commands. Scout is pulling at the harness and Mr. Carlson looks a little off balance, but they quickly cross the lawn in front of the school. My teacher is wearing khaki pants, a long-sleeved white shirt, and a tie with an exploding volcano on it. He must have a huge tie collection. He looks tired. There are dark circles under his eyes.

"I wasn't sure if you were going to be here," Mr. Carlson says.

"I was thinking the same thing about you," I say. "Did you two do your homework yesterday?"

Mr. Carlson grins. "We practiced obedience lessons in the front yard until we wore a patch of grass down to nothing. Also, you should have seen the mess I made when I tried to change Scout's bandage."

I glance down. The gauze on the dog's paw is a little uneven, but it looks clean and secure.

"You did a good job," I say.

"And it only took an hour," Mr. Carlson says. "But you're right. I did it. It's a start."

I open the door and follow the pair inside.

"Scout, halt," Mr. Carlson says.

We come to a stop in the front lobby.

"This is the part of the school I know best. I know how to get to the office, the library, my classroom, and the cafeteria. I got lost trying to get to a conference in Room 312. That's back in the new wing, near the computer lab."

"I've never been there." I snatch a piece of paper from a table in front of the office. "We can use this map."

"Maggie," Mr. Carlson says. "A paper map doesn't help me."

Duh. "You need a map you can feel, don't you? I saw one at the guide-dog school. It had raised lines on it."

"That's a tactile map. We feel the outlines to learn where the rooms, halls, doors, and windows are located in a building. They make them for towns, college campuses, ski runs, and golf courses, too."

I trace the corridors on the paper map with my fingertip. "I could make a tactile map of this. It would be easy. I could use Popsicle sticks or tooth-picks."

Scout's tail sweeps back and forth over the floor. Mr. Carlson thinks about it for a moment, then nods.

"That would be great," he says. "The art teacher has some supplies you could use."

"Excellent! But first we have to learn how to get to that conference room." I consult the map. "We need to walk down to the library and take a left."

"We can do that. Forward, Scout."

We weave our way through the school, getting a few curious glances from kids who are here early to work on the school newspaper or go to band practice. Mr. Carlson concentrates, trying to picture the way the school is laid out.

Scout picks up the pace a bit and pulls on the harness. Should I say something? Scout pulls harder. He's walking too far ahead, making Mr. Carlson lean. Mr. Carlson stumbles over a bump in the carpet. I reach out to steady his arm.

"Hang on, hang on," Mr. Carlson says in frustration. "Scout, halt."

We stop. Mr. Carlson looks like he's silently counting to ten, the way Gran does when she's mad.

"Do you really think this is going to work? One week and we'll be fine?" he asks me.

"Absolutely," I say. "Scout has started to form some bad habits. They can crop up quickly. He knows you like to walk fast, and you don't correct him to keep him by your leg. He's dragging you." I remember back to what it felt like to walk with Nugent with my eyes closed. "I bet it's harder to feel the position of the handle when he's out so far in front."

"It is. It makes me feel out of control. I need to

make him heel. We worked on 'Right' and 'Left' a lot yesterday. I should have thrown in a few 'Heels,' too." He takes a deep breath. "Thanks, Maggie. We're under control. Where to next?"

"We're coming up on a right turn and then a staircase."

"Scout, right," Mr. Carlson says firmly.

We all round the corner and start up the stairs. Scout starts to pull ahead again.

"Scout, heel," Mr. Carlson quickly commands.

The dog pauses, then walks in the correct position by his master's leg.

"Ahem," I say.

"Good dog, Scout," Mr. Carlson says.

"Good job, Mr. Carlson," I joke. "Up one more flight, and take a right at the top of the stairs."

Scout guides perfectly.

"Here we are," I say. "The conference room."

Mr. Carlson puts his hand out and feels the raised numbers on the sign that hangs by the door. "Excellent," he says. "That wasn't so bad. Thanks, Maggie. You've been a great help."

"Do you want me to show you how to get to your classroom?" I ask.

"No, that's OK. I know where we went wrong on Friday. I took the wrong staircase. I know how to get back. But if you want to do this again tomorrow, I'd like to learn my way around the art wing."

"I can't come tomorrow. Gran has a yoga class in the morning. How about the next day, Wednesday?"

"Perfect."

The bell rings loudly, and Scout's ears perk up.

"Here we go again," I sigh.

"What's wrong?" Mr. Carlson asks. "Don't you like your first class?"

"You're kidding, right? No offense, but I don't like any of them."

✚

Working with Scout and Mr. Carlson was a great way to start the day, but it goes downhill from there. Half of my math homework is wrong. I can't find my English essay, and I forgot my lunch. In the afternoon I drop my binder in the hall, and the entire eighth grade walks on my papers. Looking forward to seeing Scout is the only thing that keeps me going.

"Hi, Mr. Carlson!" I say as I walk into class.

Scout is sitting up next to Mr. Carlson, watching the students file into the classroom. The dog's ears are perked up and his eyes are bright. It looks like they've had a good day. It takes a lot of control for me not to say anything to Scout or sneak in a little ear scratching. But I manage. Barely.

"Hi, Maggie," Mr. Carlson answers. "Long time no see."

He pauses. "It's a joke. You're supposed to laugh."

Scout wags his tail. He likes Mr. Carlson's sense of humor.

Mr. Carlson sets a transparency on the overhead projector and turns to face the class. Scout swings around to stay on his left side.

I freeze in place. Will he do it?

Mr. Carlson bends over slightly and pets his dog's head. "Good boy," he says quietly. Scout leans his head against Mr. Carlson's hand and closes his eyes slightly. He loves the attention.

Yes! One small step taken!

"Take your seats, please," Mr. Carlson tells the class. "Get out a piece of paper and a pencil." He flips on the projector. Ten vocabulary words and four questions glow on the screen.

"It's the first pop quiz of the year," Mr. Carlson says. "I hope you studied your notes this weekend."

The class groans.

A pop quiz?

How can he do this to us? How can he do this to me? Why didn't he tell me this morning?

I stumble to my desk and dig a piece of paper out of my backpack. I'm not the only one who is upset. The room sounds like a nest of angry hornets.

"That's enough now—quiet down," Mr. Carlson says loudly. "This is middle school. You are responsible for going over your notes after every class. Please get started."

And here I was thinking he was a good guy, different than the other teachers! They're all the same, trying to trick us into making mistakes.

✚

I scribble my name at the top of the paper and write out the first definition:

OPTIC NERVE: a nerve in your eye
RETINA: _____

Um, I know the retina is in the eye, too. Mr. Carlson's retinas don't work—that's why he can't see. But what is the definition?

I glance over at Scout. He sees me staring at him and raises his left eyebrow. It reminds me of Gran. German shepherds have been bred to be smart. I bet Scout could pass this quiz with one paw tied behind his back.

CORNEA: _____

Oh, darn, darn. What's that?

PUPIL: _____

I thought I studied my notes. I read them, I know I did. If that's not the right thing to do, then what is? And I looked at these vocab words, too. PUPIL. It's a part of the eye. I am a pupil with two pupils. I wonder if he'd give me credit for that? PUPIL. It has a "pup" in it. PUP-IL. PUP-ILL—that makes me think about sick puppies.

Stop it! Get a grip!

I need a map to get my mind back to taking this quiz. Maybe I need a map to the Land of Studying for Tests, too.

The girl next to me puts her pencil down. She's done already?

"Five more minutes," Mr. Carlson says.

Five minutes? Argh!

I race through the quiz, trying to write down words that sound important and scientific. I sure hope he doesn't grade for spelling.

"Pass your papers forward," Mr. Carlson says. He takes another transparency out of a file folder and puts it on the overhead projector. "Today, we'll see how the brain deals with signals sent to it by the eye and other sensory organs. It's really cool. You'll love it."

Right.

He starts to talk about neurons and synapses and chemicals. The girl next to me is writing all this down. I know I should, too, but my brain hurts. It's been a really long day, and all I want is a nap.

I wish I knew how to study. I'd love to finish quizzes five minutes before everybody else. I wish I could like school. It's no fun hating it, being afraid of failing all the time, feeling trapped. I see the way kids look when they get good grades. That's how I feel when I win a basketball game, only school is more important than basketball.

I don't know why I even try. What's the use? Unless Mr. Carlson knows how to give brain transplants, I'm stuck with this one.

My pencil stops taking notes about nerve cells. It draws dogs instead—German shepherds, basset hounds, frisky black Labs—all having their chins scratched, their heads patted, or their necks rubbed.

Scout lies motionless next to Mr. Carlson's desk. I bet he's sound asleep. Told you he was smart.

Finally, the bell rings. Most of the kids take off

before the bell stops. I move more slowly, cramming my notes, my textbook, and my binder into my backpack. My head still hurts. Quizzes give me a headache.

The door bangs open. David, Brenna, Zoe, and Sunita stride in. Scout scrambles to his feet, and Mr. Carlson stands up.

"Have no fear, Wild at Heart is here!" David announces.

EIGHT

Seeing my friends snaps me out of my pop-quiz gloom. They glance curiously at Mr. Carlson and Scout, then join me by the windows. They heard about my teacher and his dog on Saturday, after we got home from the guide-dog school.

Zoe scans the cages on the counter. "We have to clean *all* of those before the late bus leaves?" she asks. "We'll never get it done."

"Sure we will," I say. "I've got it figured out. There's a big cardboard box in the back of the room. If we put the animals in there temporarily, we'll each be able to take a cage. We'll be done in no time."

"We should keep an inventory," Sunita says in her most practical tone of voice. "We don't want any of them to chew through the cardboard and escape."

75

"What happens if they eat each other?" Zoe asks, eyeing the fat guinea pigs.

"They won't," Brenna says as I set the box on the ground by the window. "These are all herbivores, well-fed herbivores. The only thing in danger of being eaten is a stray carrot."

David helps me move the animals to the box, and we start to "freshen up" the cages, putting in clean shavings, washing out food dishes and water bottles, and wiping down the exercise wheels, toys, and glass walls.

"I've never held a gerbil before," Sunita says as she cups a gray one in her hand. The gerbil twitches its nose and studies her. "They really have personality, don't they?"

"They're much better than the chicks we hatched in third grade," David says as he lets a hamster run up his arm. The hamster perches on his shoulder, half-hidden under his hair. "They don't peck. I like that."

"How's your teacher?" Brenna asks quietly, pointing with her chin to where Mr. Carlson is sitting.

I roll my eyes and whisper, "I thought he was great. Until the pop quiz."

"Already? That's harsh!" Brenna says as she picks up the rabbit and smooths her silky coat.

"You know what they say around here," I say with a fake smile. "It's middle school—get used to it."

Sunita looks at me sympathetically. "If it makes you feel better, Maggie, I had two quizzes today. One in social studies and one in math. I'm sure you did fine."

"Ha," I say. "Fat chance."

"Any news about Shelby and the missing wedding ring?" David asks. "You weren't on the bus this morning."

"Do we have to talk about that now?" Zoe asks as she refills a water bottle. "It's disgusting."

"He's sort of, um, stopped up," I explain. "No ring, no nothing. He's not eating. I think he misses the boys. Gran says we just need to give it time. That lizard is eating, though. You saw him—Iggy—the one who was raised on cat food? He figured out that spinach is good stuff. Gran is really happy about that. She sent him home with half the vegetables in our refrigerator."

"Thank heavens she gave them the *cabbage*," Zoe says. She makes it sound like cabbage is the nastiest thing on the face of the earth, and everybody laughs. The sound makes me feel at home, and I relax.

"I never knew cleaning cages could be so much

fun," Mr. Carlson calls from his desk.

"We're talking about some Wild at Heart patients," I explain.

"It sounds like you all like it there," he says.

"Are you kidding?" Brenna asks. "We love it!"

Mr. Carlson pushes away from his desk and stands up. Scout leaps to his feet instantly and looks up at his companion, waiting for a command. Mr. Carlson grasps the harness. "Scout, forward."

They walk toward us carefully. Scout pauses in front of a chair that wasn't pushed in properly. Before anyone can say anything, Mr. Carlson reaches out, finds the chair, and pushes it out of the way.

I'm still mad at him about the quiz, but I want him to succeed.

"Good dog," I whisper. *Pet him.*

"Good dog," Mr. Carlson says. He hesitates, then crouches down and gives Scout a little pat.

I'd love to see a big hug and lots of ear scratching and fur ruffling, but I guess these things take time. A little pat is a good start.

"You look like a pro, Mr. C.," I say.

"Thanks, Maggie," he replies.

Scout leads my teacher the rest of the way. When they are standing next to the counter, Scout stands perfectly still. His nostrils flare and he sniffs, picking up the smells of mouse, rabbit, gerbil, hamster, and guinea pig. He seems a little confused, maybe because the cages are empty. He looks around, then freezes—there they are! A box full of scampering furry things.

I hold my breath. What's he going to do?

"What's got his attention?" Mr. Carlson asks, feeling a little tug on the harness.

"We have the rodents in a holding box on the floor," Sunita explains. "Should we move it?"

Mr. Carlson bends over and strokes Scout's back. "Good boy!" he says. "Look, but don't chase. I think he'll be OK. He was trained not to react to other dogs and cats. Maybe that's what he thinks they are—small cats."

Sunita's eyes grow wide at this insult to cats everywhere. But she doesn't say a word. I know the way she works. Some time over the next year, she'll find an excuse to visit Mr. Carlson and deliver a report on the hundred ways cats are *not* rodents. Just thinking about it makes me chuckle.

"Are they in good shape?" Mr. Carlson asks.

"Pretty good," Brenna says. "A couple of them need to have their teeth or nails trimmed. Maggie said Dr. Mac was going to take care of that."

"Here," David says, holding out a hamster.

"Want to hold one?"

"Sure," Mr. Carlson says. "What color is it?"

"Sort of a yellow-goldish color," David says. "It likes to hide."

"Oh, it's Einstein," Mr. Carlson says. "The classroom animals are all named after scientists."

"That figures," David says. He sets the hamster into Mr. Carlson's hands.

My teacher slips the tiny creature into the pocket of his shirt, then reaches in and scratches the hamster between the ears. "The janitors and the substitute who had my class last year have been taking care of them."

Einstein delicately sniffs Mr. Carlson's fingertips, then crawls to the top of the pocket and sniffs the curls of his beard. Scout wags his tail and pants a bit, then lets out a soft whine.

"Shh, Scout, it's OK," Mr. Carlson says. "It's just a hamster. We like hamsters."

He puts a hand down to pet Scout, who jumps up a little on his back paws. He whines again and licks Mr. Carlson's hand.

"What's gotten into you?" Mr. Carlson asks.

"He's drooling and his tail is down," I explain. "I think he's confused. He knows he shouldn't act up, but I think he's jealous. Maybe he shouldn't be so close to the box."

"OK, boy, you're a good boy," Mr. Carlson says gently to his dog. "Scout, back."

They step backward, away from the box of animals. That seems to calm Scout a bit.

"One more minute," Mr. Carlson continues. "Just sit nicely for one more minute. The hamsters won't hurt you."

I set some fresh cardboard tubes in the mice cage. "Are you going to correct our quizzes this afternoon?"

"No, not now," he answers. "I'll do that when my reader comes over tonight."

"What's a reader?" Brenna asks.

Mr. Carlson lifts the hamster to his shoulder. "A reader is someone I pay to read students' work to me. That's the one thing technology hasn't mastered yet—handwriting."

The hamster on Mr. Carlson's shoulder sniffs at his ear. "That tickles," Mr. Carlson laughs as he reaches up for Einstein.

"Hnnn, hnn," Scout whines.

"OK, Scout, we'll leave the rodents alone and get back to work." He hands Einstein to David. "You'd better take this little guy."

"Rowff!" Scout barks suddenly.

The startled hamster leaps out of David's hands and lands on a desk, then hops to the chair and onto the floor. It scrambles between Zoe's legs.

"Look out!" she shrieks. This frightens the rabbit, which jumps out of Brenna's arms and streaks past Scout. Brenna lunges after the rabbit, stumbles, and knocks over the cardboard box that holds the rest of the animals.

"Rowff, rowff!" Scout barks and lunges forward. He pulls Mr. Carlson off balance. Mr. Carlson stumbles, tripping over Scout and stepping on his sore paw. Scout yelps in pain.

"They're getting away!" Zoe yells.

"The door," Mr. Carlson shouts. "Close the door!"

Hamsters head for the door, gerbils run under the desks, and the mice run in twenty different directions. Everyone shouts at once.

"Get them!" hollers Brenna.

"Look out!" warns Sunita.

"Under the desk!" says Zoe.

"Don't step on them!" I caution.

"Rowff, rowff!" Scout barks.

"Scout, no! Scout, sit!" scolds Mr. Carlson.

"The door, get the door!" yells Brenna.

"Shoot! The hamsters are running down the

hall," David reports from the doorway. "Oh, no, you don't!" He closes the door just before the rabbit leaps to freedom. He picks her up. "Got one!"

"A mouse ran over my foot!" screams Zoe.

This is crazy. I stick two fingers in my mouth and whistle long and hard. It sounds like a referee's whistle in the middle of a game.

Everybody freezes and looks at me. I love whistling like that.

I take a deep breath. "Calm down, everybody."

"But what about . . ." Brenna starts.

"Good idea, Maggie," Mr. Carlson interrupts. "I'll take Scout outside. He needs a walk, and it will be easier to capture the runaways without him. It's OK, Scout, forward."

Scout glances once at the guinea pig scurrying under the blackboard, but he leads Mr. Carlson out to the hall. David gets the door for them, then grabs a box and goes out into the hall himself, in search of hamsters.

"How are you going to find them?" asks Sunita.

David waggles his eyebrows. "I'll listen for the screams," he says.

✚

It takes almost a half hour to round up the animals.

The hardest to catch are the mice. They can squeeze into the tiniest places. David finds every single hamster, even the one that caused a little excitement in the chorus room. By the time Mr. Carlson comes back, everything is calm. Most of the animals are in their cages, and a few are in the box that I'm going to carry back to Wild at Heart.

"We found all of them!" I say triumphantly.

"Thank goodness," Mr. Carlson says with a big sigh. "I was pacing back and forth on the soccer field, trying to figure out how to explain this to the principal. Lie down, Scout."

Scout looks under the desk suspiciously, as if he expects the rabbit to pounce on him, but the rabbit is safely in her cage, exhausted by the excitement. He settles down with a groan. Poor Scout. What a day.

"Can I check his paw?" I ask Mr. Carlson.

"Please," he says. He bends over and slips off Scout's harness.

I kneel and gently pet Scout before unwrapping and examining the reinjured paw. The dog looks up at me, his eyes a little sad. What does he think of the changes he's been through? He was with his foster family, then he went to the school for training, then he met Mr. Carlson and started coming here.

I'm sure he can sense that Mr. Carlson isn't one-hundred-percent comfortable and confident yet. Does Scout think he's not a good guide dog?

I scratch between Scout's ears and rub his neck. He smiles and pants a little.

"Hang in there," I whisper. "Don't give up on Mr. Carlson. He's trying."

"How is the paw?" Mr. Carlson asks.

"The cut didn't reopen, but it's tender and swollen," I report. I rewrap the bandage. "Can you let Scout take it easy this afternoon?"

Mr. Carlson nods. "I was going to work on lesson plans for the rest of the day anyway. Scout can be a couch potato."

"That's just what he needs."

"We had better get going," Sunita says. "The late bus leaves in a few minutes."

"Thanks for your help," Mr. Carlson says.

"We're sorry . . ." I start.

"Don't worry about it," Mr. Carlson says. "I'm a middle-school teacher, remember? We're trained to expect the unexpected. I appreciate all your help."

He still seems a bit uneasy. I think that this bothered him more than he wants to let on.

"Do you still want us to come back?" Brenna asks as she picks up her backpack.

"I'm counting on you," Mr. Carlson assures her.

I put on my backpack and pick up the covered box of animals. I am *so* ready to go home. As the others file out the door, I pause.

My quiz is lying on the top of a pile of papers. I had forgotten about it with all the excitement.

The sight of it makes me feel queasy.

NINE

Brenna and Sunita have to help Zoe groom a pair of poodles, and David is stuck with receptionist's duty. I carry the box of little animals in to Gran for a checkup.

"Who do we have here?" Gran asks as she dries off her hands with a paper towel.

"These are some of Carlson's Critters," I explain. "I brought home the ones that looked like they needed a little vet care."

"Hmm," Gran says, putting on her glasses and peering into the box. She lifts out the gold-colored hamster.

"That's Einstein," I say.

Gran examines him, then chuckles. "Einstein is outrageously healthy," she says. "He just needs his teeth trimmed a bit."

Like many rodents and rabbits, hamsters' teeth

can get long if they don't grind them down naturally on their food and the playthings in their cages. Gran opens Einstein's mouth, makes sure his tongue is out of the way, and trims his teeth with a small pair of clippers. I don't mind clipping dogs' toenails, but I hope she never asks me to do rodent teeth.

The trimming takes only a minute. Then Gran hands Einstein over to me.

"There are two more hamsters in the box," I say. "Newton and Copernicus. They need manicures. Or pedicures. Whatever you call it when hamsters need their toenails trimmed."

Gran quickly trims the tiny hamster toenails. "They are escape artists," she warns as I put them in the cage with Einstein. "Make sure that top is secure. Who's next?"

She reaches into the box and pulls out a fat yellow guinea pig with a band of white fur around its middle.

"Galileo," I say.

"Ahh," Gran says with a knowing look in her eyes. She cuddles Galileo and checks out his eyes and ears. "Galileo was an astronomer, among other things. He supported the theory that planets revolve around the sun, not the earth. That scared lots of people—they weren't ready for the new idea. He was a brave man."

She examines the guinea pig's tiny limbs. "Galileo also became blind late in his life. I see . . . the foot," she says.

I nod. Galileo's front right foot looks infected and sore.

"That's easy enough to treat," Gran says as she pulls some antibiotic cream out of a drawer.

I take Galileo from Gran and hold him snugly against my chest so that she can spread the cream on his sore foot.

"Mr. Carlson must really care for these little guys," she says.

"He's used to tiny critters. He said something about growing up in an apartment. He was never allowed to have a dog, but he had lots of rodents. If you ask me, I think dogs make him nervous. Do you think he was afraid of Scout at first?"

Gran watches the way Galileo limps across his cage, unhappy with the goo on his foot.

"No, not afraid," she says. "The trainers at the guide-dog school would have noticed. But he has had a lot of adjusting to do—first, to his blindness, and second, to relying on a dog, an animal he doesn't have much experience with."

Getting used to an awesome dog like Scout would take me about three seconds, but I'm not Mr. Carlson.

Gran cracks her knuckles and stretches her fingers. "You know, Scout has made a lot of adjustments, too. Even though he has been training his whole life to work with a blind human, every situation is different. He has to get used to the way Mr. Carlson gives commands, and also to his house and to the school."

Scout has to get used to school? I hadn't thought about that before. I've thought about it for me, maybe, but for Scout? Still, it's a school with lots of kids, teachers, and funny smells from the cafeteria. Scout sees new kids every class period, I guess, kids who are big and loud. Lockers slam, the bell rings every forty-five minutes. That's a big change from guide-dog school. I wonder if Scout feels as crowded as I do in the halls. I bet he worries about keeping Mr. Carlson safe.

"Let's finish up here," Gran says, peering at the last residents of the box. "Five mice?"

"One of them has a sore eye," I say. "But I figured you should look at all of them in case it was an infection that could spread to the others."

"That was smart," Gran says.

An unexpectedly warm feeling passes over me. I haven't been feeling very smart today. The comment seems extra nice coming from Gran.

She looks at each mouse, checking from nose to tail. The fifth one, a female, has a swollen eye, but it turns out to be a piece of a wood shaving, not an infection. Gran flushes it out easily and puts the mouse in a glass cage with the others.

"I don't like the idea of you taking the animals on the bus again," she says as she watches the mice run around the cage. "I can drive you on Wednesday morning if you want. Tomorrow I have my yoga class. Are you going to help Mr. Carlson map out the school again?"

"I think so," I say. *Unless I got a D or F on that quiz and he decides to get someone else to help him.* I crouch down to watch the little mouse with the sore eye. She scurries to hide in a toilet-paper tube. I wish I could hide like that.

"So, how was school today?" Gran asks, looking at me with those laser-beam eyes.

"Lots of things happened at school," I say as I watch the quivering mouse. I know I'm stalling, but it's the truth. Lots of things *did* happen.

I'm saved from more questioning by a knock on the door.

"Come in," Gran says.

It's Zoe. "Dinner's about ready. It's going to be spectacular."

"That meat loaf smells great," Gran says.

I take a sniff. She's right. All of a sudden, I'm starving.

Gran takes a pen out of her pocket. She has to write up the reports about Carlson's Critters. "Maggie, run in and set the table," she says. "I'll be only a couple of minutes. We'll have a nice dinner, and then you'll have lots of time to work on your homework. I thought Mr. Carlson said something about a quiz coming up soon."

Zoe pauses. "They had that quiz today," she says innocently. "Maggie told us all about it. Sunita had two quizzes. I'll probably have one tomorrow. My English teacher had that look on her face."

Thanks a lot, Zoe!

"You didn't mention the quiz to me, Maggie," Gran says.

"I, uh, just forgot," I say. "It's so hard to keep everything straight, plus we had the great escape after school. We get our grades tomorrow. It's not a big deal."

TEN

Mr. Carlson has passed back our quizzes. I feel like someone just slapped me in the face.

My grade? A whopping forty-nine percent.

I go cold. Forty-nine percent? That's not just failing—that's *flunking*.

There is so much red on the page that it looks like a Christmas decoration. I got three out of ten definitions right for twelve points. The questions about how the eye works were worth sixty points. It's a good thing Mr. Carlson gave partial credit. I got thirty-seven.

I redo the math in the margin of my paper. Maybe he made a mistake.

$12 + 37 = 49$.

Nope. I flunked.

My stomach feels awful, like it has hamsters running around in it. It always feels like this when I get a bad grade. Not even one week of school has passed, and I've already dug myself into a hole.

There is a note written across the top of the paper: SEE ME AFTER CLASS.

Mr. Carlson stands in front of the board. "Most of you did quite well on the quiz," he says. "Congratulations."

The girl sitting next to me beams. I sneak a peek. She got a ninety-eight percent. I turn my quiz over so that she can't see it.

"Some of you had trouble," Mr. Carlson continues. "I'll be meeting with you to discuss the quizzes later. If necessary, we can have a make-up class during study hall. I want to make sure you understand this information. Now"—he claps his hands together—"let's get to work!"

He turns on the overhead projector. "Today we start the circulatory system. Everybody, please take out your notebooks and be ready to take notes."

I dig out my notebook and slam it on my desk. Scout looks at me, but I don't care. I don't care about anything.

There is a drawing of the heart projected on the screen. "The heart is the muscle that drives the circulatory system," Mr. Carlson says. "It has four chambers: the left ventricle and left auricle, and the right ventricle and right auricle. Blood flows to the right ventricle through two large veins. It is pumped away from the heart to the lungs via the pulmonary artery."

The girl next to me writes all this down.

"Please draw this diagram of the heart," Mr. Carlson says as he taps the projector. "Use your colored pencils to show the oxygenated blood and the nonoxygenated blood, just like in the picture."

I cross my arms and slump low in my seat. He's like all the other teachers. He doesn't know what it's like for me. He doesn't care.

The rest of the class crawls by at a snail's pace. Mr. Carlson talks about blood and vessels and getting oxygen from the lungs. Some of this stuff I know from listening to Gran. Most of it I tune out. I'm only in seventh grade. Is it going to be like this all the way through high school? And what about college? I'm never going to get in with Ds and Fs. I can forget about vet school. You have to do a good job in college before they'll let you in there.

Scout snores gently under Mr. Carlson's desk. I watch the tip of his tail twitch every once in a while as if he's dreaming. He wakes up when the bell rings and walks over to join Mr. Carlson.

My classmates quickly gather their things and get up to leave. The girl next to me puts her colored pencils away, then flips through the pages of diagrams she drew and notes she took. My notebook is empty. I didn't write anything.

Who cares? It wouldn't matter if I drew the most beautiful heart in the world. I'd still screw up the next quiz. I grab my notebook and backpack and head for the door. I am going home.

"Maggie MacKenzie," Mr. Carlson calls.

I hesitate. I could walk out, pretend I didn't hear him.

He turns off the projector and gathers the transparency sheets. The other kids from class file past me, chattering, joking, acting like life is fine. Part of me wants to follow them. But, no. I'm J.J. "No Fear" MacKenzie's granddaughter. I can't sneak out.

I turn around and walk back to my seat. Scout wags his tail happily.

"I'm here," I say.

"I'll be with you in a minute." Mr. Carlson shuffles the transparencies into a neat pile.

He pulls out the file drawer of his desk, feels the Braille labels on the file folders, and puts the transparencies into the right file. Then he and Scout walk down the aisle to where I'm sitting. Mr. Carlson sits in the desk next to me. Scout lies down in the aisle between us.

"Good boy," Mr. Carlson says, ruffling the fur on the dog's head.

He is doing a good job of praising Scout, but I don't feel like telling him that.

"We need to talk," he says.

"Yeah," I answer. I pick at a hangnail on my left thumb.

"It's not just the quiz," he continues. "You didn't take any notes in class today."

"How do you know?" I exclaim.

"It was easy to tell that you weren't writing anything down or turning pages. And you didn't ask any questions. That's not like you."

OK, so he's observant.

"You want to tell me what's up?" he asks quietly.

I bite at the hangnail. "No."

Scout scratches at his neck with his hind foot and then shakes his coat. I glance at the bandage on his paw. It looks good.

"Don't you think Scout needs to go out?" I ask.

"No," Mr. Carlson answers. "I took him out before your class started. He's fine. It's you I'm worried about."

"Don't bother," I say. I peel the hangnail back

too far, and it bleeds a little. "Look up my grades from last year. I stink at school. No reason why your class should be any different."

Mr. Carlson stretches out as far as he can in the cramped chair. "Well, yes, there is a reason. I don't let my students give up."

"I didn't give up! I studied!"

"I believe you," he answers calmly. "But you didn't study enough, or you didn't study the right way. And what you did today—not taking any notes, ignoring what was going on in class—that's the sign of a kid who has quit on herself."

"I'm not a quitter!" I swallow hard. This hangnail really hurts. It's throbbing.

"You quit today. And you act like you've already given up on the rest of the year."

"What do you care?" I ask angrily. "You don't know what it's like for me. I hate reading. I read a paragraph, and by the end of it, I can't remember a thing. I look at a test and I blank out. Elementary school was hard. Middle school is impossible. Everything has changed. I can't deal with it. The only thing I'm good at is taking care of dogs."

I pause to wipe away the tear that trickles down my face. Stupid hangnail. It hurts so much I'm crying. I sniff. My nose is running, too.

Mr. Carlson gets up and walks to his desk, using his hands to lightly feel his way down the aisle. He leaves Scout with me. I sniff again. I hate feeling like this!

Scout creeps forward and puts a paw on my sneaker. He looks up at me with his trusting eyes, like he can see and understand everything I'm going through.

I'm losing it, big time. I blubber more—big boo-hoos and a rain of tears. How humiliating, crying like this in front of a teacher. I put my arms down on my desk and hide my face. I wish the earth would open up and swallow me.

Mr. Carlson taps my shoulder and hands me some tissues.

"Thanks," I mumble.

He takes the seat again. "Scout, sit."

I can hear Scout sitting up and the sound of buckles being unfastened.

"Go ahead, boy."

And then a cold, wet nose presses against my cheek. Scout gives me a big kiss, licking away my tears. I wrap my arms around his neck with a sob, fresh tears spilling onto his fur. He holds still for a minute as I catch my breath, his tail beating against the floor to the rhythm of my heartbeat.

I finally take a deep breath and let go. I sit up and blow my nose.

Scout's guide-dog harness is on the floor. Mr. Carlson took it off so that the shepherd could comfort me. I try to swallow the large lump in my throat.

"Thanks," I croak and dry my eyes. "I really needed that."

"I thought so," he says. "Good boy, Scout."

Scout smiles, his tongue hanging out the side of his mouth. I reach out and scratch his chest. He closes his eyes. *That feels good*, he's saying. He turns his head and licks my hand.

I take a shaky breath and laugh. "OK, OK, I'm all right now. Enough kisses."

"Feeling better?"

"Yeah," I say hoarsely.

"Good. Let's start over. Tell me what's going on."

"Do you have a couple of hours?" I try to joke.

"Take all the time you need."

I pet Scout's back, and he leans against my knees. "Here goes."

For the next hour, I talk. I tell Mr. Carlson everything—what I'm good at, what's hard. How school was fun when I was a little kid but got worse when I got older. How it makes Gran sad that I don't like to read, and how she worries about my grades.

About the way Zoe flies through her homework and Sunita does extra credit for fun. How I got grounded from the clinic last year and about my tutor and all the work I put in to bring my grades up before the final report card last year.

Mr. Carlson listens carefully. He asks a few questions, but mostly he lets me ramble.

I talk about feeling lost in middle school and how everyone seems bigger and smarter than me—how they all have it together and I'm falling apart.

"When I was seven years old, I climbed too high in the oak tree that grows in our backyard," I say. "I slipped and caught hold of a branch. I hung there for ages, screaming my head off, worried that I would slip and fall. I could feel my fingers going numb. I was going to let go and fall. I knew I'd break a leg. That's what middle school feels like. I'm just barely hanging on, and I'm going to crash."

Mr. Carlson strokes his beard. "I know exactly what that feels like. And a young friend convinced me to hold on tight, that things would get easier if I kept working. Remember the map you offered to make for me yesterday, the tactile map?"

I blush. "I'm sorry, I haven't had a chance—"

He cuts me off. "No, don't worry, I understand. It's just that I was thinking about maps. You need one. A map to get you through middle school."

"You aren't talking about a map made out of toothpicks, are you?"

He shakes his head. "No, I'm talking about a plan. You need a plan, a map, customized for Maggie MacKenzie. You're right. Things are only going to get more complicated from here on out. Your teachers will expect you to do more work and to do it faster. And I suspect you'll want some free time to work at the clinic and play sports."

"You've got that right."

Mr. Carlson picks up the guide-dog harness and slips it over Scout's head. "Some kids make the adjustment to middle school with no problems. They make it look easy. But most of the kids I know stumble over something. They lose friends, they get cut from a team, or they run up against a tough subject for the first time. There are all kinds of obstacles. You need some help learning to get around them."

He buckles on the harness. Scout is back on the job.

"I'd like to meet with your grandmother and your guidance counselor," he says. "You should be there, too. Together we can put together a map for you. We'll do whatever it takes—arrange for extra help during study hall, help you with study skills, test your reading skills. You aren't stupid, Maggie. You just need a guide."

Scout wags his tail, brushing it against my leg. This is making sense.

"Let me ask you a question," Mr. Carlson says as he stands. "What happened the day you dangled from the branch of the oak tree?"

I ball up the tissues in my hand. "Gran heard me. She ran out into the backyard and got there just as I let go of the branch. I wound up crashing into her instead of the ground."

"She caught you?"

"She caught me," I agree.

"We're here to catch you, Maggie. Your grand-mother, me, Scout, your other teachers, your friends—we won't let you fall, or fail. But it's up to you, too. You have to make an effort. You can't quit."

I look at him out of the corner of my eye. I toss the tissue ball at the wastebasket. It goes in. A good start.

"OK. I promise, I'll try."

ELEVEN

I am sleepy when Gran drives me to school the next morning. Sleepy, but proud. I had a busy day yesterday.

Einstein, Galileo, and the rest of Carlson's Critters are stowed in a carrying crate in the back of the van. On my lap rests a poster board covered with a maze of toothpicks, a tactile map of the middle school. Zoe helped me with it after school yesterday. And hiding in my backpack are my notes about the circulatory system. Gran helped me write them up last night.

Gran slows the van to a crawl as we enter the fifteen-miles-per-hour zone in front of the middle school. A beige Mercedes passes illegally, then cuts in front of us. The driver is yapping into a cell phone and studying a notepad on his steering wheel.

"Look at that idiot!" Gran exclaims. She blows

her horn. "He's going to cause an accident!"

The traffic light in front of the school turns yellow, then red. The Mercedes driver slams on his brakes and screeches to a halt. Gran stops behind him and honks her horn again. She rolls down the window and leans out. "Hang up the phone!" she yells.

The bad driver glares at her in his rearview mirror. Gran glares back. The man looks away, but he keeps talking on the phone.

"I'll call the chief of police," Gran mutters, drumming her fingers on the steering wheel. "He owes me a favor." She turns to me. "We saved his toy poodle, remember?"

Gran doesn't mind pulling strings to stop bad things from happening.

"Hey," I say, pointing to the corner. "There's Mr. Carlson and Scout."

After stepping down from the bus idling on the other side of the intersection, Mr. Carlson and Scout pause at the crosswalk. Scout checks to make sure that all the cars are stopped, and Mr. Carlson listens carefully. The road is clear.

I glance at the clock on the dashboard. "They're early today," I say. "I'll have time to show Mr. Carlson the map."

They step off the curb.

"I'll come in with you," Gran says. "You can't carry the box of animals and the map. I'll set up the meeting with your guidance counselor, too."

"Sure," I agree. We had a long talk last night about my quiz grade and my middle-school problems. Gran agreed with Mr. Carlson, which was good. I'm going to have a whole team pulling for me.

The guy in the Mercedes dials his cell phone again and props it between his ear and shoulder. Mr. Carlson and Scout are crossing in front of his car. The driver glances down at the notepad on his steering wheel. He must think the light has changed—he's not looking. The car moves forward.

He's running the light—he doesn't see them!

"Look out!" I scream.

Gran leans on her horn. "Dear God!" she gasps.

I cover my eyes. There's a thud, a shout, a yelp of pain, and then . . .

Silence.

Gran pulls the van over to the side of the road and is out the door before I dare look. When I do, I see her kneeling over Mr. Carlson and Scout, who are lying in the middle of the road. The driver of the Mercedes stands next to his car, staring at what his stupidity just caused. He is still holding his cell phone.

The noise starts up. Horns honk, people shout, car doors slam. People come from all directions to help.

I run over, too, my heart pounding.

Are they . . . ?

My teacher and his dog are sprawled in the middle of the crosswalk. There is a little blood on Mr. Carlson's forehead, but Scout looks fine. Except his eyes are closed and he's not moving. Gran puts her fingers on Mr. Carlson's wrist to check his pulse. His eyes flutter and open.

"What happened?" he asks weakly.

"Don't move," Gran warns. "You were in an accident. I'm Dr. MacKenzie, your vet. You were crossing the street in front of the school, and you were hit." She glances angrily in the direction of the Mercedes. "Lie still. Help is coming."

"Scout? Where's Scout?" Mr. Carlson says.

"He's right next to you," Gran says. "I'll take care of him."

The principal and school nurse sprint toward us from the school. An ambulance siren wails in the distance. Word spreads fast.

"Maggie, get me the big red equipment box and

the small orange one in the back of the van. And I'll need two blankets."

I dash back to the van, open the sliding door, and gather what Gran needs. By the time I return, the school nurse is talking quietly to Mr. Carlson while she checks his vital signs. He seems dazed.

"Here," I say as I set the supplies next to Gran. She is studying Scout but hasn't touched him yet. "Can I help?"

"Hang on," Gran says. "I need to muzzle Scout before we do anything else." She flips open the large medical kit and takes out a bandage roll. She quickly loops some bandage around Scout's long nose.

"He won't bite you!" I protest.

Gran ties the bandage in a knot behind Scout's head. "Any dog can bite if he's in pain or frightened, Maggie. You know that."

The ambulance pulls up, and a police car parks behind it. Two medics start to examine and talk to Mr. Carlson. The police officer walks over to the driver of the Mercedes, whose cell phone has mysteriously disappeared.

"Take down Scout's vitals," Gran instructs as she tosses me a pad of paper and pen. She feels for the dog's pulse under his hind leg.

"Heart rate, one-forty."

She uses a stethoscope to listen to his lungs. "Respiratory rate, forty-five."

The numbers aren't great, but he's alive.

Gran peeks at Scout's gums, pressing them with her fingertip and seeing how long it takes for the blood to refill. She feels the bones in his legs, his ribs, and his spine.

"We have to get him to the clinic, stat," Gran says. "I don't think he's broken anything, but there might be internal bleeding."

Internal bleeding is bad. If we can't find the source and fix it, he could bleed to death.

Gran spreads one of the blankets on the street next to Scout. "When I say three, help me move him."

I put my hands under Scout's hips.

"One, two, three!"

Gran and I lift at the same time and move Scout to the blanket. Gran quickly covers him with the second blanket. His body temperature is dropping because shock is setting in. When an animal goes into shock, his blood pressure drops. If the shock is severe, like after being hit by a car, it can kill.

The ambulance attendants are fitting a big collar around Mr. Carlson's neck. He tells them he's fine and that he doesn't want to go to the hospital, but they think he needs to be checked out.

"But, Scout," he protests. "I can't leave him."

"It's OK, Mr. Carlson," I say over my shoulder. "It's Maggie. Gran is going to take him back to the clinic. She needs to check him out, too, just like you."

The attendants help my teacher sit up, then stand. He looks very pale, and there is a giant lump on his forehead. As the medics help him into the ambulance, Gran gets two men who are standing on the sidewalk to help carry Scout to the van. They lay the dog on the floor between the seats.

"Can I sit with him?" I ask Gran as I get into the van.

"Buckle your seat belt, and don't touch that muzzle," she says. She gets in the driver's seat and turns the key in the ignition. "And pray we don't hit any red lights."

TWELVE

It takes only ten minutes to get to the clinic, but it feels like forever. Scout's condition is getting worse. He's breathing in short, shallow pants. Gran said not to touch him, so I don't know what his pulse rate is. It could be racing or dropping. I'm trying to stay positive—he's awake, he's alive. We'll save him. We've *got* to save him.

Finally, we're home.

Gran turns into the driveway of the clinic, the wheels of the van squealing. She blares the horn to alert Dr. Gabe, who comes running. I slide the side door open as Gran cuts the engine. She dashes around the side of the van.

"He's still breathing," I say.

Gran quickly takes his pulse. "His heartbeat is fast and thready. Let's get him inside."

Dr. Gabe peers into the van. "What do we have

here?" he asks.

Gran climbs into the van and grabs one end of the blanket on which Scout is lying. "Get the other end," she instructs. "I'll fill you in while we carry him."

Yikes! I've never seen Gran in such a hurry with a patient.

Dr. Gabe grips the other end of the blanket. "One, two, three!" he says. Gran shuffles forward, bent over, and Dr. Gabe steps backward. They carefully maneuver Scout out of the van and carry him across the parking lot.

"Two-year-old healthy male shepherd, hit by car," Gran says. "Shocky, probable internal bleeding. The car wasn't moving too fast, but it threw him to the ground. Possible head injuries."

I run ahead and hold the door open as the two vets rush their patient into the clinic. When a dog is hit by a car, every second counts.

They carry Scout through the door and straight back to the operating room. As they lay him on the table, Scout's eyes open, then close.

No!

Gran listens to his chest with her stethoscope. "Heart is getting weaker."

Dr. Gabe peels back Scout's upper lip to look at his gums.

"Very pale," he says grimly. He presses a finger against the gum, then releases the pressure. "Capillary refill time is slow," Dr. Gabe reports. "He probably has internal bleeding. I'll tap his belly with a needle and see if we get any blood."

"Hang on!" Gran rubs her fingers on Scout's ears and touches the bottom of his foot pad. "His extremities are cool. We'll start with fluids and oxygen to stabilize him."

"Right," Dr. Gabe says. He pulls the equipment cart over and snaps on a pair of latex gloves.

Gran looks over her glasses at me. "Maggie, I need I.V. bags. Get me one sodium chloride and one Ringer's."

"On my way," I say.

As Gran wheels over the oxygen canister, I grab the bags out of a cupboard at the end of the room. The sodium chloride and Ringer's solution will help Scout's body fight off the effects of the shock and bring up his blood pressure. You have to treat the shock before you can deal with anything else.

I run the I.V. bags over to the table. An oxygen mask has been looped over Scout's snout. Dr. Gabe has the electric clippers going. He shaves the fur off Scout's foreleg, swabs the bare skin with antiseptic, and quickly inserts a catheter that he connects to the I.V. bag. The fluids are flowing instantly.

"Pulse?" he asks.

"Still one hundred and forty—very weak," Gran says. She opens Scout's eyelid and flashes a small light. "Pupils are normal. That's one good sign. Let's get a blood-pressure reading."

Dr. Gabe has already shaved the fur off the other foreleg. He hooks the monitor onto the skin and watches the green screen.

"That's way too low," he says.

Gran's eyes dart over to me. I know this is bad.

I grip the edge of the table and squeeze as hard as I can. *Come on, Scout! Fight!*

"Dopamine," Gran says. Dr. Gabe runs to the medical cupboard and pulls out a small vial of medicine. "Maggie, I need his temp. Can you do that?"

I nod. The thermometer is on the equipment cart. I pick it up, lift Scout's tail, and insert the thermometer. I watch the second hand on the clock over the door.

Dr. Gabe hands the bottle of dopamine to Gran. She sticks the needle of a syringe into the rubber top of the bottle and carefully measures out the dose. She sets the bottle on the table and injects the medicine into the catheter.

"That should bring up his blood pressure," Gran

explains. "What is his temperature?"

I pull out the thermometer. "Ninety-eight degrees." That's low. It should be one hundred and one. The shock causes body temperature to go down, too.

"Blankets, Maggie," Gran says.

I quickly yank some blankets out of a cupboard and cover Scout.

Dr. Gabe has been monitoring Scout's vital signs. "Heart rate and blood pressure are getting better."

You can do it, Scout! Come on!

Gran checks Scout's gums again. "The oxygen is helping," she says. "Capillary refill time is faster."

I walk around the side of the table. I hold Scout's paw in my hand. This is the paw that Mr. Carlson accidentally stepped on. There is no bandage on it today. The cut has healed.

My heart feels like something is squeezing it. I stroke the paw gently, hoping that makes Scout feel a little better.

Wait a minute.

"Gran, feel this," I say. "His paw is warming up."

Gran touches his foot pads and ears.

"B.P. is much better," Dr. Gabe says happily.

Scout blinks his eyes and tries to lift his head.

"Shh, shh, take it easy," Gran says as she soothes

him. "Welcome back, Scout."

His tail thumps once. I swallow hard. He's over the first hurdle—we've stabilized him. Will he make the next?

✚

Gran gently feels along Scout's body while Dr. Gabe monitors his vital signs. Scout whimpers, and Gran grimaces. She hates to cause any animal pain, but she has to know where he hurts. She feels along all his bones and tests to make sure he has feeling in his legs. Next she uses her stethoscope to check Scout's heart and lungs again and to listen for bowel sounds along his belly. She feels his belly with her fingertips several times. When she stands up and drapes the stethoscope around her neck, her face is grim.

"Time to zap some rads?" Dr. Gabe asks. He's great at taking X rays.

Gran nods. "I want to see if there are any fractured ribs. I think there is a diaphragmatic hernia, too, but we'll know better once we see the pictures. Let's give him an analgesic before we start."

Dr. Gabe injects Scout with the painkiller. It starts to work in seconds, and Scout relaxes a little. Gran turns off the flow of oxygen and removes the mask. Then they pick up the blanket that Scout's lying on and walk back toward the X-ray room.

"Can I watch?" I ask.

"No, Maggie," Gran says over her shoulder. "Fetch those little critters out of the van. They should be in the house."

The critters! I can't believe I forgot about them. And it's hot out today.

I hurry through the clinic and out the front door. *Whew!* We left the windows and the sliding door open. That's good. If they had been closed, the van would have heated up quickly. I don't want to think about what could have happened. I'm already shaken up enough by what happened to Scout.

By the time I get the critters stowed away in an empty exam room, Gran and Dr. Gabe are looking at X rays on the light box on the operating-room wall. Scout is resting on the operating table.

"He's still stable," Dr. Gabe assures me. "His blood pressure and pulse oxygenation are good, considering what happened."

I look at the X rays. "How bad is it?" I ask quietly.

"Ugly," Gran says. She points to an X ray with her pen. "Three fractured ribs. I'm pretty sure there is internal bleeding. That could mean a ruptured spleen or liver. We have to deal with that right away. He's also got a tear in the diaphragm. I don't think you've ever seen one of those before."

I shake my head.

Gran uses herself as a model, placing her hand below her ribs. "Between the chest and the abdomen, we have a layer of muscle."

I feel my own belly and nod my head.

"Those muscles protect all the soft organs inside—the intestines, the liver, and the spleen, among others. When the car hit Scout, the force tore open the muscles. Some of the stuff that should be nicely tucked in Scout's abdomen is now up in his chest. He can't expand his lungs properly to breathe. We have to get in there, repair any organ damage, stop the bleeding, and put everything back where it belongs."

"That sounds like a lot. Is he up for surgery right now?"

Gran turns and studies her patient. "His heart wasn't damaged, and neither was his head—both good things. His left lung is a little beat-up from the force of the impact, but it's not punctured or collecting fluid. And he is young and very strong, which helps his case."

"It sounds like you're going to say 'But,'" I say.

"But there's a chance he won't make it. You've seen this before, Maggie. When a car hits a dog, the dog often loses. We're going to operate and hope for the best."

Hope for the best?

I blink back the tears. Scout has to make it!

THIRTEEN

While Gran and Dr. Gabe scrub up for surgery, I lean over the operating table and quietly talk to Scout.

"OK, Scout, this is going to be hard, but I know you can do it," I whisper. "Mr. Carlson is counting on you."

Scout blinks his eyes slowly. He has a lot of painkillers in his system. Can he understand what I'm saying?

"I'll map it out for you," I continue. "Step one, you make it through surgery. Step two, you recover. Step three, you go back to work. Don't give up."

"Hnnnn, hnnnn," Scout whines.

I stroke his head. "Shhh, shhh . . . ," I say.

I glance over at the heart monitor. His other vital signs are a little weaker, but his heart is beating steadily.

"How's he doing?" Dr. Gabe asks as he prepares the anesthesia machine.

I try to smile, but can't. "We have to save him," I say.

Dr. Gabe nods. He knows how serious this is.

He secures a face mask over Scout's muzzle and starts the anesthetic. It mixes with oxygen and flows through a clear tube to the mask. Scout takes a breath of the mixture and closes his eyes. The anesthetic puts him in a special kind of sleep so that the docs can operate on him without causing any pain. Before they start, Dr. Gabe will put a plastic tube into Scout's windpipe to deliver the oxygen and anesthetic.

Gran walks over. "Are you going to watch, Maggie?"

"I want to," I say. Some kids would have a hard time watching surgery, but I grew up with it. Still, Gran always asks, just in case I'm not up for it, especially if I know the patient really well.

"OK," Gran says. "You know what to do."

I give Scout a quick kiss on the top of his head, then hurry over to the sink. While Dr. Gabe shaves the fur off Scout's belly and washes the skin with antiseptic, I pull scrubs on over my clothes, wash every single germ off my hands, and pull on a pair of latex gloves. There can't be any germs around during an operation.

When I walk back to the table, Scout is mostly covered by blue-green surgical sheets. There is one opening in the sheets, a little frame around his belly where Gran is going to operate. She is busy swabbing the area with orange antiseptic.

"Maggie, wipe this sweat off my forehead, will you?" she asks. "It's mighty warm in here."

I grab a gauze pad from the cart and sponge off Gran's face.

"Thanks." She reaches for a scalpel and stops. "Did you hear the bell?"

"Yeah," Dr. Gabe says. "That's odd. We don't have any appointments on the book."

There's a knock on the operating-room door.

"Get that," Gran tells me. "It better not be somebody trying to sell us magazines."

I open the door a crack. "Yes?"

"How is he? Can I see him?"

"Mr. Carlson!"

My science teacher is standing outside the operating-room door. He has a bandage on his forehead, and his left arm is in a sling. In his right hand, he's carrying a long white stick, the kind of cane blind people use to help them walk safely. He looks very pale and seems to be in a little bit of pain.

"Are you OK?" I gasp as I step into the hall and close the door to the operating room. "Oh my gosh, you should be at the hospital. Look at you, your arm, your head!"

"I'm fine," he says in a hoarse voice. "They let me go. I have a sprained elbow and a bump on my forehead. Scout was the one who took the blow. Tell me, please, is he . . . ? Did you . . . ?"

"Mr. Carlson, he's alive. Gran is operating on him right now."

My teacher exhales deeply and leans against the wall. "Thank heavens," he says. "How is he? Can I see him?"

I don't know what to say. Gran is always totally honest about her patients' chances. She says it's important for people to know the truth.

"Hang on for one minute," I tell Mr. Carlson.

I slip back into the operating room and hurry over to Gran.

"Mr. Carlson is here," I say. "He came straight from the hospital. He wants to come in."

"We don't let family members of patients observe surgery," Gran says.

"It's all right," Mr. Carlson calls from the door-way. "It's not like I can see what you're doing."

Gran and Dr. Gabe exchange glances over their surgical masks. They shake their heads simultaneously. They need to concentrate on what they are doing.

"That won't work," I say. "The docs need to be alone."

"Of course," Mr. Carlson murmurs.

"Let's go to the kitchen," I suggest. "Follow me."

We walk down the hall to the waiting room.

"This door connects the clinic to the house," I explain. Mr. Carlson sweeps his cane in front of him to feel where the door is. He steps into the kitchen. I describe the room to him.

"This is the oldest part of the house. Gran had a wall knocked down to make it huge. You can sit at the kitchen table or on the couch. I vote for the couch. It's to your left."

Mr. Carlson finds the couch and gingerly lowers himself to sit. He must be awfully sore.

"Can I get you anything?"

"Just a glass of water."

I bring the water and set it on the table in front of him. I sit down in the recliner. Mr. Carlson doesn't touch the water. He stares in the direction of the fireplace.

"His chances are . . . ," I start, fumbling for the

right words. "Gran and Dr. Gabe, they are great vets . . . Scout is strong."

"It's OK, Maggie," Mr. Carlson says. "I know it's bad. Your grandmother will do her best."

Toenails click across the kitchen floor as Sherlock Holmes waddles toward us. He looks at me, looks at Mr. Carlson, then heaves himself up onto the couch.

"Sorry," I say, getting up from the chair. "That's my dog, Sherlock Holmes. I'll shoo him away."

Sherlock scowls at me and half-crawls into Mr. Carlson's lap.

Mr. Carlson reaches out and pets Sherlock's head. "Can he stay? I like having him here."

"Sure," I say. "If you want."

Zoe's dog, Sneakers, dashes into the room and leaps onto the couch. He settles in on the other side of my teacher.

"That's Sneakers," I say.

"He can stay, too."

Socrates, Gran's majestic tabby cat, saunters in last. He does not jump onto the couch. He settles next to the empty hearth, where he can watch everything. Then he closes his eyes and purrs.

"You've made some friends," I say.

"Are they always like this?" Mr. Carlson asks. He

has one hand on each dog.

"Only with the people they like," I say. "I think they can tell when someone is hurting. And you might think this is silly, but I think they can make you feel better, too."

"That's not silly at all," Mr. Carlson says. "In fact, it makes sense."

He scratches Sherlock's floppy ears. "A strange thing happened to me, right after we were hit. It shocked me, actually. My first thoughts were about Scout—was he alive, was he hurt, how could I help him . . ."

"That's not shocking," I say. "That's normal."

"Not for me, not until now. I had been thinking of Scout as another tool, like a replacement for this cane or my computer. That's not what they taught us at the guide-dog school, but I couldn't help it."

His cheeks redden. "Maybe that was the real reason I was thinking about returning him. I didn't feel connected to him."

"The accident changed that?" I ask.

He takes a sip of water and sets the glass back on the table. "I realized how much he means to me. He's not a tool. He's my companion."

Mr. Carlson's voice cracks a bit, and he stops to clear his throat.

"He's my friend. In the ambulance, and then in the emergency room, I kept reaching for him. Not so much because I wanted him to guide me—they wouldn't let me walk anywhere until they took some X rays—but to feel him near me. I wanted to know he was OK. I need him. I think he needs me, too."

I can't say anything. What will Mr. Carlson do if Scout dies?

✚

"He's waking up," Gran says from the doorway.

"How is he?" Mr. Carlson asks.

Gran hesitates. "He lost a lot of blood, and there was internal damage. We're having a hard time getting him to wake up. I'm afraid he might be slip-ping into a coma."

"Come on," I say, tugging Mr. Carlson's hand. I've seen animals in this situation before. I think I know what to do.

I lead my teacher down the hall to the recovery room. Scout is lying on a heated pad on the floor, covered with a thin blanket. He still has an I.V. bag connected to his catheter and is hooked up to the machines that monitor his heart and lungs.

I guide Mr. Carlson to his dog. He kneels down

and gently strokes Scout's head. He bends close to the dog's ears and whispers so softly that I can't hear him.

In the background, Gran and Dr. Gabe talk quietly. They have done everything they can with surgery and medicine.

I can see only my teacher and his dog. Mr. Carlson smooths Scout's face, his soft ears, the dark fur that sweeps away from the corners of his eyes.

Mr. Carlson talks a little louder. "Come on, Scout, fight it, come back to me. We're a team. I can't let you go."

I glance at the monitor. The heart rate is slower. Scout is nearly motionless, his chest barely rising and falling. Dr. Gabe steps out of the room. Gran studies the floor. The heart rate slows a bit more. We're losing him.

I remember Mr. Carlson's diagram of the chambers of the heart. I think all four of my chambers are breaking.

"Scout, come back," Mr. Carlson pleads. "We've got things to do, places to go. I need you, buddy."

I can't stand it. I look away to where the tip of Scout's bushy tail pokes out from under the blanket. I'm waiting for the heart monitor to stop beeping, the silence that means the end.

The tail swishes an inch.

It swishes again, a little more.

I blink. I rub my eyes.

"I'm right here, Scout," Mr. Carlson murmurs. "I'm not leaving you."

The tail swishes back and forth. I glance at the machine. Scout's heart rate is up, and his blood pressure is rising.

"Look!" I shout.

Gran crosses the room. Scout opens his eyes, sees Mr. Carlson, and tries to lift his head.

"He's back!" I shout.

Gran fights a smile, trying to stay professional. "Don't scream in the recovery room, Maggie. It disturbs the patients."

✚

Once Scout's condition is stabilized, we creep outside to give Scout and Mr. Carlson some privacy. Dr. Gabe wanders off to write up the surgery report, whistling happily. We walk to the kitchen, where Gran starts to make a pot of coffee. She pours in the water, measures out the coffee into the basket, and turns on the coffeemaker.

"He's going to pull through, isn't he?" I ask.

Gran shakes her head in amazement and chuckles

softly. "Yes, Maggie, I think he is."

"Will he be able to guide again?"

"I'd say the chances are pretty good. It will take a month or two for him to recover. I hope James will be able to get by with his cane."

I hop up on the counter. "He can do that easily. But he'll miss Scout."

"I'll call the guide-dog school and let them know what happened," Gran says. "Once Scout's injuries have healed, they'll probably give him a little retraining. Scout has a very strong personality, and he really adores your teacher. They're going to be a team for a long time."

I swing my legs. Everything has happened so fast. I need the world to slow down for a few minutes so that I can figure it all out.

"Something wrong, Maggie?"

"I thought he was dying, Gran. I know he was. I saw the monitors."

She glances at the coffeemaker to make sure it is turned on, then turns to face me.

"Scout heard his companion's voice and decided to fight. Love is the strongest thing in the universe. It makes us do things we never thought possible."

She stops. Gran doesn't talk like this very much. "Stupid machine," she mutters, bending down to look at the coffeemaker again. "It's slower than molasses in January going uphill backwards."

"Mr. Carlson realized that he loves Scout, too. He said he had been thinking of his guide dog as a tool, like his cane. The accident made him see things differently."

"That makes sense," Gran says.

"YES!" Dr. Gabe bursts through the kitchen door holding up something gleaming and gold in his hand. His other hand holds a leash attached to our friend Shelby, who looks mighty proud.

"Mrs. Donovan's wedding ring," Gabe announces.

"It's about time," Gran says, giving Shelby a quick pat. "Gabe, why don't you give Mrs. Donovan the call she's been waiting for."

Gabe and Shelby leave, and Gran turns back to the coffeemaker. "Oh!" She smacks her forehead with the palm of her hand. "Talk about seeing things differently—it's unplugged!"

She shakes her head and reaches over to plug in the coffeemaker's electrical cord. "Get down from the counter," she scolds mildly. "Why don't you make us some sandwiches. Then I'll drive you back to school."

I open my mouth to whine and plead for the rest of the day off—but I stop.

I think about the promise I made to Mr. Carlson that day in the classroom. And I remember what John from the guide-dog school said: "Big changes are easier to handle if you know people love you." I have Gran, Sherlock, my friends, even Zoe, plus Mr. Carlson and the other folks at school.

I look at Gran and simply say, "OK."

Puppy Raising

By J.J. MACKENZIE, D.V.M.

WILD WORLD NEWS—Guide dogs are loyal and dependable, but they start out as frisky, unpredictable pups. So the guide-dog schools rely on puppy raisers. These special families volunteer to take a puppy into their household and give her basic training, love, and care until she is old enough to learn the skills she needs to become a guide dog.

Special delivery. Most guide-dog schools breed  puppies for their programs—usually German shepherds, Labrador retrievers, or golden retrievers. When a new litter of guide-dog puppies is born, the school contacts a family from its list of puppy raisers and places the pups in a home. Then it's up to the raisers to turn the eight- to twelve-week-old pups into mature, well-behaved dogs ready for guide-dog school.

Continued on page B6

New Species of Dog
Discovered in Eastern

Continued from page B1

Raise with praise. Puppy raisers teach their dogs basic commands and good manners. A guide-dog puppy must be trained with love and affection. Praise, not punishment, is the way to a dog's heart. Her raisers always praise her with hugs and kisses. They don't reward her with food. A guide dog's favorite reward is making her companion happy. When she goes back to school, her instructors will focus on what she does right, not what she does wrong.

On the town. The most important part of puppy raising is socializing the dog. That means exposing her to as many people and situations as possible. She needs to be comfortable wherever she goes. Her raisers walk her down busy sidewalks, past noisy construction sites, on city or school buses, up and down escalators, and through airports. Guide-dog puppies wear special vests to let people know they are in training. They are usually allowed to go places that other dogs can't. Some guide-dog puppies even accompany their raisers to school or work.

Check up. The guide-dog school will have some-one check on the puppy's progress every month or so to make sure she's on track. And puppy raisers are required to take their pups to the vet for frequent exams. Puppy raisers may also attend "puppy club" meetings to learn tips and talk to other raisers.

Saying good-bye. This is the hard part. After a year of love and play, the raisers must return the dog to the guide-dog school. It is time to let her go. She's old enough now to learn the skills she needs for her job. On the turn-in day, the raisers drive back to the school and hand her over.

It can be very hard for raisers to give up the dog they love. She has become part of the family. But knowing that the dog will change a blind per-son's life by giving him independence and dignity helps ease the pain of good-bye.

Back to school. At the school, the young dog goes through a number of medical tests. She'll also be tested to see if she can follow basic commands. If she passes her medical exam and obedience test, it's time to start special training to be a guide dog.

She'll spend four months learning how to guide a blind person safely through streets and buildings. At the end of the four months, she will be paired with her blind companion. They will spend another month at the school learning how to work together. Then they'll go home to start their new life.

Career change. Not all trained puppies become guide dogs. The demands on a guide dog are heavy, and not all dogs can cope with them. Some dogs are trained for other kinds of work, such as drug detection for police departments or therapy visits to the elderly. If the school decides that the dog isn't right for any kind of work, she is adopted by a loving family. Her puppy-raising family is given the first chance to adopt her.

Retirement. Guide dogs work with their blind companions for an average of ten years. They retire when they start to slow down and show signs of age. Sometimes the blind companion keeps his old dog as a pet. If not, the dog goes back to the school. There are long lists of families eager to share their homes with retired guide dogs.

DO YOU HAVE
PUPPY-RAISER POTENTIAL?

Answer these questions with your family.

1. Can someone stay home with the pup all day?

   YES   NO

2. Can someone walk and socialize the pup every day?

   YES   NO

3. Will the pup have time to sleep during the day?

   YES   NO

4. Will the pup be allowed to spend time inside?

   YES   NO

5. Will someone be able to take the pup to training classes and to the vet on a regular basis?

   YES   NO

6. Returning the dog after raising her can be hard. Do you think your family could handle it well?

   YES   NO

If you answered YES to all of these questions, your family may have puppy-raising potential! Check the yellow pages or search the Internet for guide-dog schools and puppy-raising organizations in your area.

About the Author

Chris Whitney/Doylestown, PA

Laurie Halse Anderson has had many pets—dogs, cats, mice, even salamanders. Her best dog was a German shepherd named Canute. She got him from a shelter when he was two years old. Canute was Laurie's constant running companion. He helped her get into shape for a half-marathon. A few summers ago, he died in her arms. She keeps his collar in her office for inspiration while writing.

Laurie has written many books for kids, including picture books and a young adult novel. When she's not writing or teaching writing workshops at local schools, Laurie splits her time between bird-watching and hanging out at the local vet clinic. She lives in Ambler, Pennsylvania, with her husband, her two daughters, and a cat named Mittens.